ELSIE
AT VIAMEDE

The Original

ELSIE DINSMORE

COLLECTION

ELSIE
AT VIAMEDE

Book Eighteen

Martha Finley

HENDRICKSON
PUBLISHERS

Elsie at Viamede

Hendrickson Publishers Marketing, LLC
P. O. Box 3473
Peabody, Massachusetts 01961-3473

ISBN 978-1-59856-418-1

Printed in the United States of America

Original publication date—1892

First Hendrickson Edition Printing—August 2010

Chapter First

It was a beautiful evening at Viamede—the sun was nearing his setting, shadows were sleeping here and there upon the velvety lawn, the blossoming flowers filled the air with their delicious perfume, the waters of the bayou beyond reflected the roseate hues of the sunset clouds, and the song of some oarsmen in a passing boat came to the ear in pleasantly mellowed tones. Tea was over, and the family had all gathered upon the veranda overlooking the bayou. The momentary silence was broken by Rosie's pleasant voice.

"Mamma, I wish you or grandpa, or the captain, would tell the story of Jackson's defense of New Orleans. Now, while we are in the neighborhood we would all, I feel sure, find it very interesting. I think you have been going over Lossing's account of it, mamma," she added laughingly, "for I found his *Pictorial History of the War of 1812* lying on the table in your room with a mark in that part."

"Yes, I had been refreshing my memory in that way," returned her mother, smiling pleasantly into the dark eyes gazing so fondly and entreatingly into hers. "And," she added, "I have no objection to granting your request, except that I do not doubt that either your grandfather or the captain could do greater justice to the subject than I," glancing inquiringly from one to the other.

"Captain, I move that you undertake the task," said Mr. Dinsmore. "You are, no doubt, better prepared to do it justice than I, and I would not have my daughter fatigued with the telling of so long a story, sir."

"Always so kindly careful of me, my dear father," remarked Mrs. Travilla in a softly spoken aside.

"I am doubtful of my better preparation for the telling of the story, sir," returned the captain in his pleasant tones. "But if both you and mother are disinclined for the exertion, I am willing to undertake the task."

"Yes, do, captain." "Do, papa," came in the eager tones from several young voices. Lifting baby Ned to one knee, Elsie to the other, while the rest of the young members of the household grouped themselves about him, he began his story after a slight pause to collect his thoughts.

"You all, I think, have more or less knowledge of the war of 1812–14, which finished the work of separation from the mother country so nearly accomplished by the War of the Revolution. Upon the close of that earlier contest, England, it is true, acknowledged our independence, but evidently retained a hope of recovering her control here.

"All through the intervening years, our sailors on our merchant vessels and even, in some instances, those belonging to our navy, were subjected to insults and oppression when met on the high seas by the more powerful ones of the English. The conduct of the British officers—claiming the right to search our vessels for deserters from theirs and often seizing American-born men as such—was most gallingly insulting. The wrongs thus inflicted upon our poor seamen were enough to rouse the anger and indignation of the meekest of men. The clearest proofs of citizenship availed nothing. They were seized, carried forcibly aboard the British ships, and, if they refused to serve their captors, were brutally flogged again and again.

"But I will not go into details with which you are all more or less acquainted. We did not lack abundant cause for exasperation, and at length, though ill-prepared for the struggle, our government declared war against Great Britain.

"That war had lasted two years—both parties were weary of the struggle, and negotiations for peace were being carried on in Europe. In fact the treaty had been signed, December twenty-fourth, in the city of Ghent, Belgium. But news did not travel in those days nearly so fast as it does now, and so it happened that the Battle of New Orleans was fought two weeks afterward on January eighth, 1815, both armies being still in ignorance of the conclusion of peace."

"What a pity!" exclaimed Gracie.

"Andrew Jackson was the commanding general?" asked Walter. "Was he an American by birth, Brother Levis?"

"Yes. His parents were from Ireland, but he was born on the border between North and South Carolina in 1767. He was old enough to remember some of the occurrences of the Revolutionary War—one of them being himself carried to Camden, South Carolina, as a prisoner. There he was nearly starved to death and brutally treated by a British officer—cut with a sword because he refused to black his boots for him."

"Is that so, sir?" queried Walter. "Well, I shouldn't wonder if the recollection of all that made him more ready to fight them in the next war, particularly at New Orleans, than he would have been otherwise."

"No doubt," returned the captain. "Jackson was a man of great energy, determination, and persistence. It is said his maxim was, 'Till all is done nothing is done.' In May of 1814 he was made a major-general in the regular army and appointed to the command of the Department of the South, the Seventh Military District, with his headquarters at Mobile, of which the Americans had taken possession as early as April of 1812.

"Jackson's vigilance was sleepless. The Spanish had possession of Pensacola, and, though professing neutrality, they were secretly favoring the British. Of this Jackson promptly informed our government, but at that time our War Department was strangely apathetic, and his communication was not responded to in any way.

"He had trusty spies, both white and dark-skinned, everywhere, who kept him informed of all that was taking place in the whole region around. He knew that British marines were allowed to land and camp on shore; that Edward Nichols, their commander, was a guest of the Spanish governor; and the British flag was unfurled over one of the forts. Also, he found that Indians were invited to enroll themselves in the service of the British crown, and that Nichols had sent out a general order to his soldiers and a proclamation to the people of Kentucky and Louisiana, announcing that the land and naval forces at Pensacola were only the vanguard of a far larger number of vessels and troops that were intended for the subjugation of Louisiana and especially the city of New Orleans.

"Jackson arrived in that city on the second of December and prepared to defend it from the British, whom he had driven out of Florida. They had planned to take the lower Mississippi Valley, intending to keep possession of the western bank of the river. They had among them some of the finest of Wellington's troops, who, but a short time before, had been engaged in driving Napoleon out of Europe.

"In December, twelve thousand men under the command of Sir Edward Packenham, who was the brother-in-law of Wellington, were landed below New Orleans. They had come from Jamaica across the Gulf of Mexico. Their expedition was a secret one, and they approached New Orleans midway between Mobile Bay and the Mississippi River, entering Lake Borgne and anchoring there.

"A small American navy, composed of five gunboats, opposed their progress, but it was soon dispersed by their superior force of fifty vessels, large and small. Then the British took full possession of the lake and landed troops upon a lonely island called the Isle des Pois—or Pea Island.

"Some Spaniards, who had formerly lived in New Orleans, told Cochrane of Bayou Bienvenu, at the northwestern extremity of Lake Borgne, by which he could nearly reach the city, as the bayou was navigable for large barges to within a few miles of the Mississippi River.

"A party was sent to explore and found that by following it and a canal they would reach a spot but half a mile from the river and nine miles below the city.

"They hurried back to Cochrane with a report to that effect, and by the twenty-third of December half of the army had reached the spot.

"A few months before—September first—the British sloop of war *Sophia,* commanded by Captain Lockyer, had sailed from Pensacola with dispatches for Jean Lafitte, inviting him and his band to enter the British service.'"

"Lafitte? Who was he?" queried Walter.

"A Frenchman," replied the captain, "who, with his elder brother, Pierre, had come to New Orleans some six years before. They were blacksmiths, and for a time worked at their trade. But afterward they engaged in smuggling and were leaders of a band of corsairs, seizing, it was said, merchantmen of different nations, even some belonging to the people of the United States. For that they were outlawed, though there was some doubt that they were really guilty. But they carried on a contraband trade with some of the citizens of Louisiana, smuggling their wares into New Orleans through Bayou Teche, or Bayou Lafourche and Barataria Lake. That had brought them into trouble with the United States authorities, and the British thought to get help of the buccaneers in their intended attack upon the city, where Pierre Lafitte was at the time a prisoner.

"Captain Lockyer carried to Jean a letter from Colonel Nichols offering him a captain's commission in the British Navy and $30,000. To his followers, he offered exemption from punishment for past deeds, indemnification for any losses, and rewards in money and lands if they would go into the service of England's king.

"Lockyer also brought another paper, in which they were threatened with extermination if they refused the offers in the first."

"Were they frightened and bribed into doing what the British wished, sir?" asked Walter.

"No," replied the captain. "They seized Captain Lockyer and his officers and threatened to carry them to New Orleans as prisoners of war, but Lafitte persuaded them to give that up, and they released the officers. Lafitte pretended to treaty with them, asking them to come back for his reply in ten days, and they were permitted to depart.

"After they had gone, he wrote to a member of the legislature telling of the visit of the British officers, what they had said to him and his men, and sending with his letter the papers Captain Lockyer had left with him. He also offered his own and his men's services in defense of the city, on condition that past offenses should never be brought up against them.

"Troops were badly needed in the American army, and Governor Claiborne was inclined to accept Lafitte's offer. But the majority of his officers were opposed to so doing, thinking the papers sent were forgeries and the story made up to prevent the destruction of the colony of outlaws, against whom an expedition was then fitting out. Lafitte knew of the preparations, but he supposed they were for an attack upon the British. They, the members of the expedition, made a sudden descent upon Barataria, captured a large number of Lafitte's men, and carried them and a rich booty to New Orleans.

"Some of the Baratarians escaped, Jean and Pierre Lafitte among them. They soon collected their men again near the mouth of Bayou Lafourche, and after General Jackson took command in New Orleans, again offered their services, which Jackson accepted, sending part of their group to man the redoubts on the river and forming of the rest a corps that served the batteries with great skill.

"In a letter, Jean Lafitte said: 'Though proscribed in my adopted country, I will never miss an occasion of serving her or of proving that she has never ceased to be dear to me.'"

"There!" exclaimed Lulu with enthusiasm. "I don't believe he was such a very bad man, after all."

"Nor do I," her father said with a slight smile, then went on with his story.

"Early on the fifteenth, Jackson, hearing of the capture of the gunboats, immediately set to work to fortify the city and make every possible preparation to repulse the expected attack of the enemy. He sent word to General Winchester in command at Mobile, to be on the alert and messengers to generals Thomas and Coffee urging them to hasten with their commands to assist in the defense of the city.

"Then he appointed, for the eighteenth, a grand review of all troops in front of the Cathedral of St. Louis in what is now Jackson Square, but at that time it was called 'Place d'Armes.'

"All the people turned out to see the review. The danger was great, the military force with which to meet the foe small and weak, but Jackson made a stirring address, and his aide, Edward Livingston, read a thrilling and eloquent one.

"They were successful in rousing both troops and populace to an intense enthusiasm, taking advantage of martial law and suspension of the writ of *habeus corpus*."

"What is that, papa?" asked Gracie.

"It is a writ which in ordinary times may be given a judge to have a prisoner brought before him that he may inquire into the cause of his detention and have him released if unlawfully detained. It is a most important safeguard to liberty, and it was inherited by us from our English ancestors."

"What right had Jackson to suspend it?" asked Walter.

"A right given by the Constitution of the United States, in which there is an express provision that it may be suspended in cases of rebellion or invasion, should the public safety demand it," replied the captain, then resumed his narrative.

"After the review, Jean Lafitte again offered his own services and those of his men, urging their acceptance, and they were mustered into the ranks and appointed to important duty.

"Jackson showed himself sleeplessly vigilant and wonderfully active, making every possible preparation to meet and repulse every coming foe.

"On the evening of the twenty-third, the schooner *Carolina*, one of the two armed American vessels in the river, moved down and anchored within musket shot of the center of the British camp. Half an hour later she opened a tremendous fire upon them from her batteries, and in ten minutes had killed or wounded a hundred or more men. The British answered with a shower of Congreve rockets and bullets, with little or no effect, and in less than half an hour were driven in confusion from their camp.

"They had scarcely recovered from that when they were startled by the sound of musketry in the direction of their outposts. Some prisoners whom General Keane had taken told him there were more than twelve thousand troops in New Orleans, and he now felt convinced that such was the fact. He gave Thornton full liberty to do as he would.

"Thornton moved forward and was presently met by a column under Jackson. There was some fierce fighting, and at length the British fell sullenly back. About half-past nine the fighting was over; but two hours later, when all was becoming quiet in the camp, musket firing was heard in the distance. Some drafted militia, under

General David Morgan, had heard the firing upon the *Carolina* early in the evening, insisted upon being led against the enemy, and on their way had met some British pickets at Jumonsville and exchanged shots with them. By that advance against the foe, Jackson had saved New Orleans for the time, and now he set vigorously to work to prepare for another attack, for he knew there would be another. Also, he knew that the men who were to make it were fresh from the battlefields of Europe—veteran troops not likely to be easily conquered or driven away. He omitted nothing that it was in his power to do for the defense of the city, setting his soldiers to casting up entrenchments along the line of the canal from the river to Cypress Swamp. They were in excellent spirits and plied their spades with such energy and zeal that by sunset a breast-work three feet high might be seen along the whole line of his army.

"The American troops were quite joyous on that Christmas Eve, but the British soldiers were gloomy and disheartened, having lost confidence in their commander, Keane, and finding themselves on wet ground, under a clouded sky, and in a chilly atmosphere. But the arrival of their new commander, Sir Edward Packenham, in whose skill and bravery they had great confidence, filled them with joy.

"But while the Americans were busy at work preparing for the coming conflict, the foe were not idle—day and night they were busy getting ready a heavy battery with which to attack the Carolina. On the morning of the twenty-seventh, they had it finished, began firing hot shot upon her from a howitzer and several twelve- and eighteen-pounders, and soon succeeded in setting her on fire, so that she blew up.

"It was a tremendous explosion, but fortunately her crew had abandoned her in time to escape it. The *Louisiana*, who had come down to her aid, was near sharing her fate, but, by great exertion on the part of her crew, she was towed out of the reach of the enemy's shot, anchored nearly abreast of the American camp on the other side of the river, and so saved to take a gallant part in the next day's fight. Packenham next ordered his men to move forward and carry the entrenchments of the Americans by storm. They numbered eight thousand, and toward evening the two columns, commanded respectively be Generals Gibbs and Keane, obeyed that order, moving forward and driving in the American pickets and outposts. At twilight they encamped, some of them seeking repose while others began raising batteries near the river.

"The Americans, however, kept them awake by quick, sharp attacks, which the British called 'barbarian warfare.'"

"Barbarian warfare, indeed!" sniffed Walter. "I wonder if it was half so barbarous as what they employed the Indians to do to our people."

"Ah, but you must remember that it makes a vast difference who does what, Walter," laughed Rosie.

"Oh, but, of course," returned the lad. Captain Raymond went on with his story.

"Jackson was busy getting ready to receive the enemy, watching their movements through a telescope, planting heavy guns, blowing up some buildings that would have interfered with the sweep of his artillery, and calling some *Louisiana* militia from the rear. By the time the British were ready to attack, he had four thousand men and twenty pieces of artillery ready to receive them. Also the *Louisiana* was in a good position to use her cannon with the effect of giving them a warm reception.

"As soon as the fog of early morning had passed away, they could be seen approaching in two columns, while a party of skirmishers, sent out by Gibbs, were ordered to turn the left flank of the Americans and attack their rear.

"Just then a band of rough-looking men came down the road from the direction of the city. They were Baratarians, who had run all the way from Fort St. John to take part in the fight, and Jackson was delighted to see them. He put them in charge of the twenty-four-pounders, and they did excellent service.

"Next came the crew of the *Carolina*, under Lieutenants Norris and Crawley. They were given charge of the howitzer on the right. A galling fire of musketry fell upon the British as they advanced in column, then the batteries of the *Louisiana* and some of Jackson's heavy guns swept their lines with deadly effect, one of the shots from the *Louisiana* killing and wounding fifteen men. The British rocketeers were busy on their side, too, but succeeded in inflicting very little damage upon the Americans.

"But I must leave the rest of the story for another time, for I see we are about to have company," concluded the captain, as a carriage was seen coming swiftly up the driveway. It brought callers who remained until the hour for the retiring of the younger ones among the hearers.

Chapter Second

The next evening the Viamede family were again gathered upon the veranda, and, at the urgent request of the younger portion, seconded by that of the older ones, the captain resumed the thread of his narrative.

"Keane's men," he said, "could no longer endure the terrible fire that was so rapidly thinning their ranks, and they were presently ordered to seek shelter in the little canals, where, in mud and water almost waist deep, they leaned forward, concealing themselves in the rushes which grow on the banks. These were Wellington's veterans, and they must have felt humiliated enough to be thus compelled to flee before a few rough backwoodsmen, as they considered Jackson's troops.

"In the meantime, Gibbs and Rennie were endeavoring to flank the American left, driving in the pickets till they were within a hundred yards of Carroll and his Tennesseeans in an effort to cut Rennie off from the main body of the enemy by gaining his rear. Henderson went too far, met a large British force, and he and five of his men were killed or several wounded. But Gibbs, seeing how hard the fight was going with Keane, ordered Rennie to fall back to Keane's assistance. Rennie reluctantly obeyed, but only to be a witness of Keane's repulse. Packenham, deeply mortified by the unexpected disaster to his veterans, presently ordered his men to fall back and retired to his headquarters at Villere's."

"Had he lost many of his men that day, sir?" queried Walter.

"The British loss in the engagement is said to have been about one hundred fifty," replied Captain Raymond. "Of the Americans, nine were killed and eight wounded. Packenham called a council of war, at which it was resolved to bring heavy siege guns from the navy and with them make another attempt to conquer the Americans and get possession of the city, which Packenham now began to see to be by no means the easy task he had at first imagined. He perceived that it was difficult, dangerous, and would require all the skill of which he was master and that his movements must be both courageous and persevering if he would save his army from destruction.

"Jackson, too, was busy with his preparations, extending his line of entrenchments, placing guns, establishing batteries, and appointing those who were to command and work them.

"A company of young men from the best families, under Captain Ogden, were made his bodyguard and subject to his orders alone. They were posted in Macarte's garden.

"Everyone was full of enthusiasm, active and alert. Particularly so were the Tennessee riflemen. They delighted in going on 'hunts,' as they called expeditions to pick off sentinels of the enemy. So successful were they in this kind of warfare on Jackson's left, very near the swamp, that soon the British dared not post sentinels there. They—the British—threw up a strong redoubt there which Captain You and Lieutenant Crawley constantly battered with heavy shot from their cannon. But the British persevered, and by the end of the month had mounted several heavy guns, with which, on the thirty-first, they began a vigorous shower of fire upon the Americans.

"That night the whole British army had moved forward to within a few hundred yards of the American lines, and in the gloom, they began rapid work with spade and pickax. They brought up siege guns from the lake and before dawn had finished three half-moon-shaped batteries at nearly equal distances apart—six hundred yards from the American lines.

"The batteries were made of earth, hogsheads of sugar, and whatever else could be laid hold of that would answer the purpose. Upon them they placed thirty pieces of heavy ordnance, manned by picked gunners of the fleet, who had served under Nelson, Collingwood, and St. Vincent.

"That morning was the first of January of 1815. A thick fog hid the two armies from each other until about eight o'clock. Then a gentle breeze blew it aside, and the British began firing briskly upon the American works, doubtless feeling sure they would presently scatter them to the winds, and that their own army, placed ready in battle array, would then rush forward, overpower the Americans, and take the city.

"Heavier and heavier grew their bombardment. The rocketeers sent an incessant shower of fiery missiles into the American lines and upon Jackson's headquarters at Macarte's. More than a hundred balls, shells, and rockets struck the building in the course of ten minutes. He and his staff immediately left the house, and in the meantime he had opened his heavy guns on the assailants.

"The British were amazed to find heavy artillery thundering along the whole line and wondered how the Americans had got their guns and gunners.

"It was an absolutely terrible fight. Packenham sent a detachment of infantry to turn the American left, but they were driven back in terror by the Tennesseeans under Coffee. After that, the conflict was between the batteries alone, and before noon the fire of the British had sensibly abated. Then they abandoned their works and fled helter-skelter to the ditches for safety, for their demi-lunes were crushed and broken—the hogsheads, of which they were largely composed, having been reduced to splinters and the sugar that had filled them mixed with the earth. Some of their guns were dismounted, others careened so that it was very difficult to work them, while the fire of the Americans was still unceasing. At noon, as I have said, they gave up the contest. That night, they crawled back and carried away some of their cannon, dragging them with difficulty over the wet ground and leaving five of them a spoil to the Americans.

"The British were deeply chagrined by this repulse, had eaten nothing for sixty hours, nor had any sleep in all that time, so that their New Year's Day was even gloomier than their Christmas had been.

"The Americans, on the other hand, were full of joy that they had been able to repulse their own and their country's foes. Their happiness was increased by the news that they were soon to have a reenforcement, Brigadier General John Adair arriving with the glad tidings that two thousand drafted militia from Kentucky were coming to their assistance. These same arrived on the fourth of the month, and seven hundred of them were sent to the front under Adair.

"Packenham had lost some of his confidence in the ability of himself and his troops to conquer the Americans, but he hoped to be more successful in a new effort. He decided to try to carry Jackson's lines on both sides of the river. He resolved to rebuild his two batteries near the levee, which had been destroyed by the Americans, mount them well, and employ them in assailing the American right, while Keane, with his corps, was to advance to fill the ditches and use scaling ladders with which to mount the embankments.

"But first fifteen hundred infantry with some artillery were to be sent under cover of night to attack Morgan, whose works were but feebly manned and so get possession, enfilade Jackson's line, while the main British army attacked it in front.

"All the labor of completing these arrangements was finished on the seventh, and the army, now ten thousand strong, was in fine spirits, no doubt thinking they had an easy task before them. But Jackson saw through their designs, and he was busily engaged in making preparations. He had thrown up a redoubt on the edge of the river and mounted it with cannon so as to enfilade the ditch in front of his line. He had, besides, eight batteries at proper distances from each other, and Patterson's marine battery across the river, mounting nine guns. Also the *Louisiana* lay near at hand ready to take any part she could in assisting him.

"The plain of Chalmette was in front of Jackson's line. His whole force on the New Orleans side of the river was about five thousand. Only twenty-two hundred of them were at his line, only eight hundred of them were regulars, and most of them were new recruits being commanded by young officers.

"The British attempted to carry out Packenham's plans, but Thornton was delayed in reaching Morgan by the falling of the water in the canal and river, so that the sailors had to drag the boats through the mud in many places. It was three o'clock in the morning before half his force had crossed. Besides, the powerful current of the Mississippi carried them downstream, and they were landed at least a mile and a half below the point at which they had intended to disembark. The roar of the cannon on the plain of Chalmette was heard before all had landed. The British formed in line and advanced to within 450 yards of the American entrenchments, and there, under Gibbs and Keane, they stood in the darkness, fog, and chilly air, listening for the boom of Thornton's guns.

"The time must have seemed long to them, and doubtless they wondered what delayed him. But day began to dawn, the red coats of the enemy could be dimly seen by our troops through the fog, and Lieutenant Spotswood of battery number seven opened the battle by sending one of his heavy shots in among them.

"The fog rolled away, and the British line was seen extending two-thirds of the distance across the plain of Chalmette. A rocket was sent up from each end of the line and it broke into fragments, the men forming into two columns by companies. Then Gibbs moved forward toward the wooded swamp, and his troops, as they advanced, were terribly pelted by the fire of the Americans of the batteries numbers six, seven, and eight pouring shot incessantly into their line, making lanes through it.

"Some sought shelter from the storm behind a projection of the swamp into the plain but in vain. Whole platoons were prostrated, but their places were instantly filled by others.

"The company who were to have brought the fascines and scaling ladders had forgotten them, and that, with the terrible fire of the American batteries, wrought some confusion in the ranks. But they pressed on bravely, cheering each other with loud huzzas, their front covered by blazing rockets. As rank after rank fell under the fire of the Americans, their places were instantly occupied by others, and the column pushed on toward the American batteries on the left and the weaker line defended by the Kentuckians and the Tennesseeans.

"Those British troops were Wellington's veterans who had fought so bravely in Europe, and now, in spite of the awful slaughter in their ranks, they moved unflinchingly forward without pause or recoil, stepping unhesitatingly over their fallen comrades, till they were within two hundred yards of our lines. Then General Carroll's voice rang out in clear, clarion tones, 'Fire!' And, at the word, the Tennesseeans rose from behind their works, where they had lain concealed, and poured in a deadly fire, each man taking sure aim. Their bullets cut down scores of the enemy.

"Then, as the Tennesseeans fell back, the Kentuckians stepped quickly into their places and poured in their fire with equally deadly aim. Another rank followed, and still another, so that fire slackened not for a moment, while at the same time grape- and round-shot from the batteries were crashing through the British ranks, making awful gaps in them.

"It was enough to appall the stoutest heart, and their lines began to waver. But their officers kept encouraging them with the cry, 'Here comes the Forty-fourth with the fascines and the ladders!'"

"Papa, what are fascines?" asked Gracie.

"Long bundles of sticks used for different purposes in engineering," he replied. "It was true they were coming, Packenham at their head, encouraging his men by stirring words and deeds. But presently a bullet struck his bridle arm, and his horse was shot under him. He quickly mounted a pony belonging to his favorite aide, but another shot disabled his right arm. And, as his pony was being led away to the rear, another passed through his thigh, killed the horse, and he and it fell to the ground together. He was carried to the rear and placed under an oak, where he soon died in the arms of Sir Duncan McDougall, the aide who had resigned his pony to him.

"Other officers fell, till there were not enough to command. General Keane was shot through the neck, and the wound compelled him to leave the field. General Gibbs was mortally wounded and died the next day. Major Wilkinson, who then took command, fell on the parapet, mortally wounded; then the British fled in wild confusion."

"But they had been very brave," remarked Gracie. "What a pity it was that they had to fight in such a bad cause. Were there very many of them killed, papa?"

"Yes, a great many. Of a regiment of brave Highlanders with twenty-five officers, only nine officers and 130 men could be mustered after the terrible fight was over. Another regiment had lost five hundred men.

"While this fighting had been going on, another of their divisions of nearly one thousand men, led by Colonel Rennie, attacked an unfinished redoubt on Jackson's right and succeeded in driving out the Americans there. But they could not hold it long, being terribly punished by Humphrey's batteries and the Seventh Regiment. Yet Rennie succeeded in scaling the parapet of the American redoubt. Beale's New Orleans Rifles poured such a tempest of shot upon the officers and men in the redoubt that nearly every one was killed or wounded. Rennie, who had just shouted, 'Hurrah, boys! The day is ours!' fell mortally wounded.

"And now this attacking column also fell back, and by hastening to the plantation ditches, sought shelter from the terrible tempest of shot and shell coming from Jackson's lines.

"General Lambert tried to come to the aid of Packenham, Gibbs, and Keane, but he was able only to cover the retreat of their vanquished and flying columns."

"The victory was won then, papa?" queried Lulu.

"Yes, though the battle had lasted but a short time. By half-past eight in the morning, the musketry fire had ceased, though the artillery kept theirs up till two o'clock in the afternoon."

"Were both Americans and British playing their national airs while the fight was going on, sir?" asked Walter.

"The British had no music but a bugle," replied the captain. "Not even a drum or a trumpet, but all through the fight from the time they sent up their first signal rocket, the New Orleans Band that was stationed near the spot where the American flag was flying played national airs both to cheer and animate the soldiers."

"Were not the British rather more successful in another part of the field, captain?" asked Eva.

"Yes," he replied, "in their attack upon the troops on the right bank of the river—they being only militia and few in number, who were also fatigued and poorly armed. Morgan, their commander, was compelled to spike his cannon and throw them into the river, his men being driven from their entrenchments.

"Then Thornton, his assailant, pushed on to Patterson's battery, three hundred yards in the rear. Patterson, threatened by a flank movement also, was compelled to spike his guns and flee onboard the *Louisiana,* her sailors helping to get her out of the reach of the foe.

"But Thornton soon heard of the disasters of his comrades on the other side of the river and received orders to join them. Jackson had sent four hundred men to re-enforce Morgan, but there was now no need of their services. Thornton re-embarked his troops at twilight, the Americans repossessed themselves of their works, and Patterson removed the spikes from his guns, put his battery in better position, and at dawn informed Jackson of what he had done by heavy firing upon the British outposts at Bienvenu's.

"In that battle of January 8, 1815, the British had lost twenty-six hundred men—seven hundred killed, fourteen hundred wounded, and five hundred made prisoners—while the Americans had only eight killed and thirteen wounded. Lossing tells us, 'The history of human warfare presents no parallel to this disparity in loss.'

"In Thornton's attack, the British loss was a little more than a hundred and the American, one killed and five wounded. On that side of the river the British secured their only trophy of their efforts to capture New Orleans. So Lossing tells us, adding, 'It was a small flag, and now hangs conspicuously among other war trophies in Whitehall, London, with the inscription: "Taken at the Battle of New Orleans, January 8, 1815."'"

"That looks as though our British cousins must esteem it quite a triumph to be able to succeed in taking anything from Uncle Sam," laughed Rosie.

"Yes," said Walter. "I think they compliment us by making so much of that one little trophy."

"So do I," said Lulu. "Is that the end of the story?"

"No, not quite," replied the captain. "After the battle had come to an end, Jackson and his staff passed slowly along his whole line, speaking words of congratulation and praise to his brave troops, officers, and men. Then the band struck up 'Hail Columbia!' Cheer after cheer for the hero went up from every part of the line. The citizens also, who had been anxiously and eagerly watching the battle from a distance, joined in the cheering. Then, after refreshing themselves with some food—doubtless having gone into battle without waiting to eat their breakfast—the soldiers set to work to bury the dead of the enemy in front of Jackson's lines and take care of the wounded.

"General Lambert sent a flag of truce asking for an armistice in order to bury his dead, and Jackson granted it on condition that the British should not cross to the right bank of the river.

"The next morning, detachments from both armies were drawn up in front of the American lines at a distance of three hundred yards. Then the dead bodies between that point and the entrenchments were carried by the Americans upon the very scaling ladders left there by the British and delivered to them. They were buried on Bienvenu's plantation, and, as Lossing tells us, the graves were still there undisturbed when he visited the spot in 1861. He says also that it is regarded with superstitious awe by all people in the neighborhood.

"The wounded who had been taken prisoners were carried to the barracks in New Orleans and tenderly cared for by the citizens. Some of the dead British officers were buried that night by torch light in the garden at Villere's, and the bodies of others, among whom were Packenham, Rennie, and Gibbs, were sent to their friends in England."

The captain paused, and Violet said playfully, "I fear we are fatiguing you, my dear. Suppose you leave the rest of your story for another time."

"Shall we have some music now?" added her mother, a suggestion that was immediately adopted, the whole party adjourning to the parlor.

Chapter Third

The captain opened the piano and glanced smilingly at his young wife. But Violet shook her head playfully. "I think mamma should be the player tonight," she said. "She has scarcely touched the piano for months, and I am really hungry to have her do so."

"Will you give us some music, mother?" queried the captain, offering to lead her to the instrument.

"Yes," she returned laughingly. "I could never willfully allow my daughter to suffer from hunger when in my power to relieve it."

"Patriotic songs, first, please mamma," entreated Walter, as she took her seat before the instrument. "I do believe we all feel like singing 'Hail Columbia!' and 'The Star-Spangled Banner.' At least I do."

"I presume we are all in a patriotic frame of mind tonight," she returned, giving him a smile of mingled love and pride as she struck a chord or two, then dashed off into "Yankee Doodle Dandy" with its many variations.

"Hail Columbia!" and "Star-Spangled Banner" followed, old and young uniting together with enthusiasm in singing the patriotic words, but still other voices were unexpectedly heard joining in on the concluding strains, "And the star-spangled banner in triumph shall wave; O'er the land of the free and the home of the brave!"

"Oh, Cousin Molly and Mr. Embury! Dick, too! And Betty!" cried Violet, hurrying with outstretched hand toward the doorway into the hall, where the cousins stood in a little group looking smilingly in upon them. "Come in. We are delighted to see you."

The invitation was promptly accepted, and for the next few minutes there was a tumultuous exchange of joyous greetings.

Dr. Percival and his half brother, Robert Johnson, had been spending some months together in Europe, their sister Betty visiting friends in Natchez through the winter, and only that morning the three had returned to Magnolia Hall. Betty made a home with her sister, Molly, and the brothers were always welcome guests.

Presently all were seated and a very animated conversation ensued, the newly arrived having much to tell and many inquiries to make concerning absent friends and relatives.

After a while it came out that Betty was engaged and shortly to be married, provided "Uncle Horace" was satisfied with regard to the suitableness of the match, of which no one acquainted with the reputation, family, and circumstances of the favored lover, felt any doubt.

It was a love match on both sides. The gentleman, an American, was engaged in a lucrative business. He had irreproachable character and reputation, pleasing appearance and manners—in fact, all that could reasonably be desired—and assured of which, Mr. Dinsmore gave a prompt consent, adding his warm congratulations, which Betty accepted with blushes and smiles.

"I was not unprepared for this, Betty," he said with a smile. "I had received a letter from the gentleman himself, asking for the hand of my niece, Miss Johnson."

"Oh, Betty, how nice!" cried Rosie with a gleeful laugh, softly clapping her hands. "When is it to be? I hope before we leave for the North, for I, for one, want to see what a pretty bride you will make, and I dare say Mr. Norris, your favored suitor, feels in as great haste as I."

"I am quite aware that I have no beauty to boast of, cuz," laughed Betty. "But I believe it's a conceded point that a woman always looks her best at such a time and in bridal attire. However that may be, though, I shall want you all present, so I will hurry my preparations in order that the great event may take place while you are here to have a share in it. By the way, I have laid my plans to have three bridesmaids and several maids of honor, and I have planned that they shall be my three young friends—Cousin Rosie Travilla, Evelyn Leland, and Lucilla Raymond," glancing from one to another as she spoke. She then added, "Now don't decline, any one of you, for I shall be mortally offended if you do."

"No danger of that, unless compelled by some one of the older folks," laughed Rosie, turning inquiringly to her mother, while Evelyn colored and smiled, hesitated momentarily, then said in a noncommital way, "You are very kind, Betty, but I'll have to think about it a little and, of course, ask permission."

Lulu's face grew radiant with delight. "Oh, Betty, how good of you!" she exclaimed. "Papa, may I?" turning a very pleading look upon him and hurrying to his side.

He took her hand in his, smiling affectionately into the eager, entreating eyes. "I think you may, daughter," he said kindly. "Since Cousin Betty is so good as to include you in the invitation. I see nothing in the way at present."

"Oh, thank you, sir!" she cried joyously, then turned to listen with eager interest to an animate discussion going on among the ladies in regard to the most suitable and tasteful attire for the bride and the bridesmaids or maids of honor.

"The bride will, of course, wear white," Violet was saying. "But it would be quite pretty and in accordance with the fashion for her maids of honor to dress in colors."

"Yes," assented Rosie. "And I propose blue for Eva, delicate straw or a canary color for Lu, who has a complexion just to suit, and pink for me. What do you say, girls?" turning to them where they stood side by side.

"I like the idea," replied Evelyn. Lulu adding, "And so do I. Do you approve, papa?" hurrying to his side again.

"Yes, daughter. If it pleases you and meets the approval of the ladies."

"You are so good to me, dear papa!" she exclaimed with a look of gratitude and affection.

But it was growing rather late, and leaving various matters to be settled in another interview to be held at an early day, the cousins bade each other a fond good night and departed.

"Papa, I do think I have just the best and kindest father in the whole world!" exclaimed Lulu, seating herself upon his knee and putting her arm about his neck, her lips to his cheek, when he had come to her room for the usual good-night bit of chat.

"Rather strong, isn't it?" he queried laughingly, holding her close and returning her caress.

"Not too strong, you dear, dear papa!" she said, hugging him tighter. "Oh, if ever I'm disobedient or ill-tempered again I ought to be severely punished."

"My dear child," he said gravely, smoothing her hair with a caressing hand as he spoke, "do not ever again give your father the pain of punishing you. Watch and pray, and try every day to grow into the likeness of the dear Master. It makes me happy that you want to please me, your earthly father, but I would have you care more about pleasing and honoring Him."

"I do care about that, papa. Oh, I want very much to have Him pleased with me, but next to that I want to please you, because you are such a good, kind father, and I love you so dearly."

"Yes, daughter, and I esteem your love one of the greatest blessings of my life, while you are dearer to me than words can express—one of God's good gifts for which I am truly thankful. But I must now bid you good night and leave you to rest, for it is growing late."

"Yes, sir. But I feel so wide awake because I'm so excited thinking about Betty's wedding and all of those affairs. So I wish you'd stay just a little bit longer. Can't you, papa?"

"No, daughter, I must leave you and you must go to bed at once. Try to banish exciting thoughts, and get to sleep."

"I'll try my very best to obey my own dear father," she returned, looking up into his face with eyes full of ardent affection.

He smiled, held her close for a moment, repeating his caresses, saying low and tenderly, "God bless and keep my dear daughter through the night and wake her in the morning in health and strength, if it be His will." Then releasing her, he left the room.

She was soon in the land of dreams, and the sun was shining when she woke again.

The wedding and matters connected with it were the principal topics of discourse at the breakfast table. Betty had expressed an ardent wish to have present at the ceremony all the relatives from the neighborhood of her old home, saying that she and Molly had already dispatched invitations which she hoped would be accepted. Now it was settled that Mr. Dinsmore and Grandma Elsie should write at once, urging all to come to Viamede and remain till the summer heats would make it more prudent to return to a cooler climate. There was talk, too, of an entertainment to be given there to the bride and groom, of suitable wedding gifts, and also the attire of maids of honor.

The young girls who were selected to take part in the ceremony were particularly interested—excitable, Lulu especially so. She could hardly think of anything else, even in the schoolroom, and as a consequence recited so badly that her father looked very grave indeed. When dismissing the others, he told her she must remain in the schoolroom to study until she could recite each lesson very much more creditably to both herself and her teacher.

"Yes, sir," she said in an unwilling tone, casting down her eyes and coloring with mortification. "I think the lessons were dreadfully hard today, papa."

"No, daughter, it is only that your mind is dwelling upon other things. You must learn to exercise better control over your thoughts and concentrate them always upon the business at hand."

"But, papa, I'll never be able to learn the lessons before dinner time, and I am hungry now. Are you going to make me fast till I recite perfectly?"

"No, my child. You may eat when the rest of us do and finish your tasks afterward. You may have a cracker now if you are hungry."

"Oh, may I go and get her some, papa?" asked Gracie, who had lingered behind the others, full of concern and sympathy for her sister, and was now standing close by his side.

"Yes, my darling," he said, smiling upon the little girl and smoothing her pretty hair with softly caressing hand.

"Oh, thank you, sir!" and away she ran to return in a few minutes with a plate of crackers. She found Lulu alone, bending over a book and apparently studying with great diligence.

"Oh, thank you, Gracie!" she exclaimed. "You are ever so good. I was so taken up with the talk about the wedding at breakfast time that I didn't eat nearly as much as usual. Some folks in papa's place would have made me fast till my lessons were learned, but he's such a good, kind father. Isn't he?"

"Yes, indeed!" returned Gracie emphatically, setting down the plate as she spoke. "Now I'll run away and let you learn your lessons."

Lulu did not feel fully prepared for her recitations when the dinner bell rang, but, having her father's permission, she went to the table with the others. At the conclusion of the meal, he inquired in an aside, his tone kind and pleasant, if she were ready for him, yet.

"No, sir," she replied, "not quite."

"You may take half an hour to digest your dinner, then go back to your tasks," he said.

"Yes, sir, I will," she answered, taking out the pretty little watch, which was one of his gifts, and noting the time. Then, in company with Rosie, Evelyn, and Gracie, she went out upon the lawn and sauntered about under the trees, gathering flowers from here and there.

She was careful to return to the schoolroom at the appointed hour. Presently her father followed her. "Are those lessons ready, daughter?" he asked in his usual kindly tones.

"If they are," he continued, "I would hear them at once and you might make one of the party who are going to Magnolia Hall."

"Papa, I should so like to go along!" she exclaimed, looking up coaxingly into his face.

"And I would be glad to give you the pleasure," he said with a slight sigh. "But you know that I cannot do that, having already told you your lessons must be creditably recited before you can be allowed any further recreation."

"They're so long and hard, papa," grumbled Lulu, looking woefully disappointed.

"No, my child. With your usual attention, you could easily have learned them before the regular school hours were over," he said. "I am not going with the others and will come for your recitation in another hour or perhaps sooner." So saying, he turned and left the room.

"Oh, dear! I do wish I was old enough not to have lessons to learn," sighed Lulu. But seeing there was no escape, she turned to her tasks again, and when her father came in according to his promise, she was able to say she was ready for him and to recite in a creditable manner. He gave the accustomed meed of praise, smiling kindly on her as he spoke. "There, daughter," he added. "You see what you can do when you give your mind to your work, and I hope that in the future you will do so always at the proper time."

"I hope so, papa. I do really mean to try," she replied, hanging her head and blushing. "Are the ladies and girls all gone?"

"Yes, some time ago," he said. "I am sorry I could not let you go with the others, as I have no doubt you would have enjoyed doing so."

"I hope you didn't stay at home just to hear my lessons, papa?" she said regretfully.

"I might possibly have gone could I have taken my eldest daughter with me," he replied. "Though there were other matters calling for my attention. However," he added with a smile, "you need not measure my disappointment by yours, as I am certain it was not nearly so great."

At that moment a servant came to the door to tell the captain that a gentleman had called on business, and he was in the library waiting to see him.

"Very well. Tell him I will be there presently," replied Captain Raymond. Then turning to Lulu, "You may amuse yourself as you like for an hour, then prepare your lessons for tomorrow."

"Yes, sir," she answered as he left the room, then she put on her hat and taking a parasol, wandered out upon the lawn.

The captain had been giving the young people some lessons in botany, and the girls were vying with each other as to who should gather into her herbarium the largest number of plants and flowers, particularly such as were to be found in that region, but never, or very rarely, in the more northern one they called their home. Lulu had found, and, from time to time, placed in her herbarium, several which she highly prized for both beauty and rarity, and now she went in quest of others.

She had scarcely left the house when, much to her surprise, she met her baby brother and his nurse.

"Why, Neddie dear, I thought you had gone—" but she paused, fearing to set the child to crying for his mother.

"Marse Ned's sleeping when dey goes, Miss Lu. I spec's dey'll be back fo' long," said the nurse. Catching him up in her arms, she began a romping play with him, her evident object to ward off thoughts of his absent mother.

Lulu walked on, spent a half hour or more gathering flowers, then returned to the schoolroom, where she had left her herbarium lying on her desk. But Master Ned, there before her, had pulled it down on the floor, where he sat tearing out the plants that she had prepared and placed in it with so much labor and care.

At that trying sight, Lulu's anger flamed out as it had not in years—not since the sad time when little Elsie was so nearly sacrificed to her eldest sister's lack of self-control.

"You naughty, naughty boy!" she exclaimed, snatching the herbarium from the floor. "I'd just like to shake you well and spank you, too. You deserve it richly, for you have no business to be here meddling with my things!"

At that the boy sent up a wail. Then their father's voice was heard from the veranda. "Come here to papa, Neddie boy," and the little fellow, who had now scrambled to his feet, hastened to obey.

Lulu trembled and flushed hotly. "I wish I'd known papa was so near, and I'd have kept my temper, too," she sighed ruefully to herself, then set to work to repair damages to the best of her ability. But soon her passion cooled, with thoughts dwelling remorsefully upon her unkind treatment of her baby brother and also apprehensively on the consequent displeasure of her dearly loved father. She loved little Ned, too, and she heartily wished she had been more gentle and forbearing toward him.

But her hour of recreation was past. With Ned's baby prattle to his father as he sat on his knee coming to her ear through the open window, she sat down at her desk, took up her books, and tried to study. But it seemed impossible to fix her thoughts upon the business at hand, and presently hearing the patter of the little fellow's feet as he ran along the veranda, then out into the garden, she sprang up and followed him.

"Oh, Neddie dear," she said, catching him in her arms and giving him a hearty kiss. "Sister is ever so sorry she was cross to you. Will you forgive her and love her still?"

"Ess," returned the baby boy with good will, putting his chubby arms about her neck and hugging her tight, then cooing sweetly, "Ned 'oves oo, Lu."

"And Lu loves you, Neddie darling," she returned, kissing him again and again.

Then setting him down, she sped back to the schoolroom, took up her book, and made another attempt to study—but without success. Laying it aside again almost immediately, she went in search of her father.

He had left the veranda, but going on into the library, she found him in an easy chair with a newspaper in his hand that he seemed to be reading with great attention, for he did not turn his head or eyes toward her as she drew near and stood at his side. She waited longingly for a recognition of her vicinity, but he gave none, seeming too intent upon his paper to even be aware of it. He had taught her that she must not rudely interrupt him or any grown person so engaged, but wait patiently till her presence was noted and inquiry made as to what she wished to say.

The five or ten minutes she stood silently waiting seemed a long time to her impatient temperament. "Oh, would papa never give her an opportunity to speak to him?" At last, however, as he paused in his reading to turn his paper, she ventured a low-breathed, "Papa."

"Go instantly to your own room, taking your books with you, Lucilla, and don't venture to leave it till you have my permission," he said in stern, cold accents and without giving her so much as a sideways glance.

She obeyed in silence. Reaching her own room, she again opened her book and tried to study. But she found herself so disturbed in mind that it was well-nigh impossible to take in the meaning of the words as she read them over and over. "I can't learn these lessons till I've made it up with papa," she sighed aloud, and putting down the book, she opened her writing desk.

In a few minutes, she had written a very humble little note, saying how sorry she was for the indulgence of her passion and her unkindness to her darling little brother; that she had asked and received his forgiveness; and then sought her father to beg him to forgive her, too, and tell him she was ready to submit to any punishment he thought best to inflict. But, oh, might it not be something that would be over before the rest of the family should come home from their drive?

She signed herself, "Your penitent little daughter, Lulu," folded the note, sealed it up in an envelope, and wrote her father's name on the outside.

She could hear the prattle of her baby brother coming from the lawn. Her window opened upon an upper veranda, and going out there, she called softly, "Ned, Neddie, dear!"

The little fellow looked up and laughed. "Lu!" he called. Then catching sight of the note in her hand, "What oo dot?" he queried. "A letter for papa," she replied. "Will you take it to him and ask him to please read it?"

"Ess. Fro it down," he said, holding up both hands to catch it. "Me will tate it to papa."

It fell on the grass at his feet, he stooped and picked it up, then trotted away with it in his hand.

Again Lulu took up her book and tried to study, but with no better success than before. "What will papa do and say to me?" she was asking herself. "Oh, I hope he won't keep me long in suspense! I don't believe he will. He never does, and—ah, yes, I hear his step."

She rose hastily, hurried to the door, and opened it. He stood on the threshold. "Papa," she said humbly, "I am very, very sorry I was passionate and cross to dear little Ned."

"As I am," he replied, stepping in, securing the door, then taking her hand, leading her to the side of the easy chair, and seating himself therein. "I was deeply grieved to hear my eldest daughter speak in such angry words and passionate tone to her baby brother. It not only gave the dear little fellow pain, but it set him a very bad example that I greatly fear he will follow one of these days—so giving me the pain of punishing him and you that of seeing him punished!"

"Papa, I am the one who ought to be punished," she burst out in her vehement way. "And I just hope you will punish me well. But, oh, please don't say I shall not go to Cousin Betty's wedding, or not be one of her bridesmaids or maids of honor."

He made no reply at first. There was a moment's silence, then she exclaimed, "Oh, papa, I just can't bear it! I'd even rather have the severest whipping you could give me."

"You are a little too old for that now," he said in moved tones, drawing her to a seat upon his knee. "It has always been to me a hard trial to feel called upon to punish my dear child in that way; a sad task to have to do so in any way; and if you are a good girl from now on to the time of the wedding, you may still accept Betty's kind invitation."

"Oh, thank you, sir! Thank you very much indeed!" she exclaimed. "I don't deserve to be allowed to, but, oh, I do fully intend to rule my temper better in the future!"

"I hope so, indeed, but you will not succeed if you try merely in your own strength. Our sufficiency is of God, and to Him alone must we look for strength to resist temptation and be steadfast in fighting the good fight of faith. Try, my dear child, to be always on your guard! 'Watch and pray,' is the Master's command, repeated again and again. 'Take ye heed, watch and pray.' 'Watch ye, therefore.' 'And what I say unto you I say unto you all. Watch.' 'Watch ye and pray lest ye enter into temptation.'"

"Papa, I do mean to try very hard to rule my own spirit," she said humbly. "I have been trying."

"Yes, dear child, I have not been blind to your efforts," he returned in tender tones. "I know you have tried, and I believe you will try still harder, and you will at length come off conqueror. I fear I have not been so patient and forbearing with you today as I ought. I think now I should have let you speak when you came to me in the library a while ago. Your father is by no means perfect, and therefore he has no right to expect absolute perfection in his children, either."

"But I had indulged my temper, papa, and I did deserve to be punished for it."

"Yes, that is true. But it is all forgiven now, and your father and his eldest daughter are at peace again," he added, giving her a loving embrace.

"That makes me so happy," she said, lifting her dewy eyes to his. "I am always very far from happy when I know that my father is displeased with me."

"You love him, then?"

"Oh, yes, yes, indeed! Dearly, dearly!" she exclaimed, putting her arms about his neck and laying her cheek to his.

He held her close for a moment, then said, "Now I want you to spend an hour over your lessons for tomorrow, after which you and I will have a walk together." And with that, he left her.

By teatime the family were all at home again, and their talk at the table that evening was almost exclusively of the preparations for the approaching wedding of Cousin Betty.

"Mamma," said Rosie at length, "I for one would dearly like to go to New Orleans and select dress and ornaments for myself and a present for Betty."

"I see no objection, if a proper escort can be provided," was the smiling rejoinder.

"Suppose we make up a party to go there, do the necessary shopping, and visit the battlefields and everything connected with them," suggested Captain Raymond. "We can stay a day or two if necessary, and I think we'll feel repaid." The proposal was received with enthusiasm by the younger portion of the family, and even the older ones had nothing to say against it. Lulu was silent, but she sent a very wistful look in her father's direction. It was answered with a nod and smile, and her face grew radiant, for she knew that meant that she would be permitted to take the little trip with the others.

"Dear papa, thank you ever so much," she said, following him into the library as they left the table.

"For what?" he asked jestingly, laying a hand upon her head and smiling down into the happy, eager face.

"Giving me permission to go with you and the rest to New Orleans."

"Ah, did I do that?" he asked, sitting down and drawing her to a seat upon his knee.

"Not in words, papa, but you looked it," she returned with a pleased laugh, putting her arm about his neck and kissing him with her usual ardent affection. "Didn't you, now?"

"I don't deny that I did, yet it depends largely upon the good conduct of my eldest daughter," he said in a graver tone, smoothing her hair caressingly as he spoke. "I hope she will show herself so sweet-tempered and obedient that it may not be necessary to leave her behind because she is lacking in those good qualities."

"Papa," she replied low and feelingly, "I will ask God to help me to be patient and good."

"And if you ask for Jesus' sake, pleading His most gracious promise, 'If ye ask anything in My name, I will do it,' your petition will be granted."

At that moment the other girls came running in, Rosie saying eagerly, "Oh, Brother Levis, we all hope you will be kind as to go on with your historical stories of doings and happenings at New Orleans. Please treat us to some of them tonight and let us have all before we visit their scenes, won't you?"

"Certainly, Sister Rose," he replied, adding, "It looks very pleasant on the veranda now. Shall we establish ourselves there?"

"Yes, sir, if you please," she said, dancing away, the others following.

Presently all were quietly seated, the older people almost as eager for the story as were the young, and the captain began.

"While the armies before New Orleans were burying their dead, others of the British were trying to secure for themselves the free navigation of the Mississippi below the city by capturing Fort St. Philip, which is in a direct line some seventy or eighty miles lower down the stream, and was considered by both British and Americans as the key of the State of Louisiana.

"The fort was at that time garrisoned by 366 men under the command of Major Overton of the rifle corps with the addition of the crew of the gunboat. Just about the time that the British who had been killed in the Battle of New Orleans were being carried by the Americans under Jackson to their comrades for burial, a little squadron of five English vessels appeared before the fort and anchored out of range of its heavy guns, the bomb vessels with their broad sides toward it. At three o'clock they opened fire on it. Their bombardment went on with scarcely a pause till daybreak of the eighteenth, when they had sent more than a thousand pounds of powder. They had sent, too, beside the shells, many rounds and grape-shot.

"During those nine days the Americans were in their battery, five of the days without shelter, exposed to cold and rain a part of the time. But only two of them were killed and seven wounded.

"On the eighteenth, the British gave up the attempt. That same day a general exchange of prisoners took place, and that night the British stole noiselessly away. By morning they had reached Lake Borgne, sixty miles distant from their fleet.

"They could not have felt very comfortable, as the wintry winds to which they were exposed were keen, and the American mounted men under Colonel De la Ronde, following them in their retreat, annoyed them more than a little.

"The British remained at Lake Borgne until the twenty-seventh, then boarded their fleet, which lay in the deep water between Ship and Cat Islands.

"In the meantime Jackson had been guarding New Orleans lest they might return and make another effort against it. But on leaving that vicinity they went to Fort Bowyer, at the entrance of Mobile Bay, thirty miles distant from the city of that name, then but a village of less than one thousand inhabitants. The fort is now called Fort Morgan.

"It was but a weak fortress, without bomb-proofs, and mounting only twenty guns, only two of them larger than twelve-pounders, some of them less. It was under the command of Major Lawrence.

"The British besieged it for nearly two days, when Lawrence, a gallant officer, was compelled to surrender to a vastly superior force.

"It is altogether likely that the British would have gone on to attack Mobile, had news not come of the treaty of peace between the United States and Great Britain.

"The news of Jackson's gallant defense of New Orleans caused intense joy all over the Union, while in England it was heard with both astonishment and chagrin."

"They didn't know how Americans could fight," said Walter with a look of exultation. "And they have never attacked us since."

"No," said his mother. "And God grant that we and our kinsmen across the sea may evermore henceforward live in peace with each other."

"It seems a great pity that the news of peace had not come in time to prevent that dreadful Battle of New Orleans and the fighting of which you have just been telling us, captain," remarked Evelyn.

"Yes," he replied. "And yet, perhaps, it may have been of use in preventing another struggle between the two nations. We have had difficulties since, but fortunately they have thus far been settled without a resort to arms."

"I suppose there was an exchange of prisoners?" Walter said inquiringly.

"Yes, though, in regard to some, the Dartmoor captives especially, it was strangely slow."

"Dartmoor, papa?" Gracie said with inquiring look and tone.

"Yes, Dartmoor is a desolate region in Devonshire. Its prison, built originally for French prisoners of war, had thirty acres of ground enclosed by double walls, within which were seven distinct prisons.

"At the close of the War of 1812–14 there were about six thousand prisoners there, twenty-five hundred of them impressed American seamen who had refused to fight against their country, having been forced into the British Navy and being still there at the beginning of the struggle. Some of the poor fellows, though, had been in Dartmoor Prison ten or eleven years. Think what an intense longing they must have felt for home and their own dear native land! How unbearable the delay to liberate them must have seemed! They were not even permitted to hear of the treaty of peace till three months after it had been signed. But after hearing of it, they were in daily expectation of being released, and just think how hope deferred must have made their hearts sick. Some of them showed a disposition to attempt an escape, and on the fourth of April they demanded bread and refused to eat the hard biscuits that were given them instead.

"Two evenings later they very reluctantly obeyed orders to retire to quarters, some of them showing an inclination to mutiny and passing beyond the limits of their confinement, when, by the orders of Captain Shortland, commander of the prison, they were fired upon. Then the firing was repeated by the soldiers without the shadow of an excuse, as was shown by the impartial report of a committee of investigation, the result of which was the killing of five men and the wounding of thirty-three."

"I hope those soldiers were hung for it!" exclaimed Walter, his eyes flashing.

"No," replied the captain. "The British authorities pronounced it 'justifiable homicide,' which excited the hottest indignation on this side of the ocean. But now the memory of it has nearly passed away."

"Now, Brother Levis, if you're not too tired, won't you please go on and tell us all about the taking of New Orleans in the last war?" asked Walter, looking persuasively into the captain's face.

"Certainly, if you wish to hear it," came the pleasant-toned reply. And all present expressing themselves desirous to do so, he at once began.

"Ship Island was appointed as the place of rendezvous for both land and naval forces, the last named under the command of Captain David G. Farragut, the others led by General Butler.

"Farragut arrived in the harbor of the island, on the twentieth of February, 1862, on his flagship, the *Hartford*, in which he sailed on the second, from Hampton Roads, Virginia, but sickness had detained him for a time in Key West.

"The vessels of which he had been given the command, taken collectively, were styled the Western Gulf Squadron. Farragut had been informed that a fleet of bomb vessels, under Commander David D. Porter, would be attached to his squadron. Porter was the son of Commander David Porter, who had adopted Farragut when a little fellow and had him educated for the Navy. It was he who commanded the *Essex* in the War of 1812, and Farragut was with him, though then only in his twelfth year."

"Then he must have been past sixty at the time of the taking of New Orleans," remarked Walter reflectively, as he calculated in his head.

"He and Porter joined forces at Key West," continued the captain. "Porter's fleet had been prepared at the Navy Yard in Brooklyn, exciting much interest and curiosity. There were twenty-one schooners of from two to three hundred tons each; they were made very strong and to draw as little water as possible. Each vessel carried two thirty-two-pounder rifled cannon and was armed besides with mortars of eight and a half tons that would throw a fifteen-inch shell which, when filled, weighed 212 pounds.

"Farragut's orders were to proceed up the Mississippi, reducing the forts on its banks, take possession of New Orleans, hoist the American flag there, and hold the place till more troops could be sent him.

"An expedition was coming down the river from Cairo, and if that had not arrived, he was to take advantage of the panic that his seizure of New Orleans would cause and push on up the river, destroying the rebel works. His orders from the Secretary of War were, 'Destroy the armed barriers which these deluded people have raised up against the power of the United States Government, and shoot down those who war against the Union; but cultivate with cordiality the first returning reason which is sure to follow your success.' Farragut, having received these orders, at once began carrying them out with the aid of the plans of the works on the Mississippi that he had been directed to take, particularly of Fort St. Philip, furnished him by General Barnard, who had built it years before.

"The plan made and carried out was to let Porter's fleet make the attack upon the forts first, while Farragut, with his larger and stronger vessels should await the result just outside the range of the rebel guns. Then, when Porter had succeeded in silencing them, Farragut was to push on up the river, clearing it of Confederate vessels and cutting off the supples of the fort. That accomplished, Butler was to land his troops in the rear of Fort St. Philip and try to carry it by assault. Those two forts, St. Philip and Jackson, were about thirty miles from the mouth of the river—Fort Jackson on the right bank and Fort St. Philip on the left.

"Ship Island, the place of rendezvous, is about one hundred miles northeast of the mouth of the Mississippi. In the last war with England, as I have told you, St. Philip had kept the British in check for nine days, though they threw one thousand shells into it.

"And Fort Jackson was a larger fortification, bastioned, built of brick, with casemates and glacis, rising twenty-five feet above the water. Some French and British officers, calling upon Farragut before the attack and having come from among the Confederates— while visiting whom they had seen and examined these forts with their defenses—warned him that to attack them would only result in sure defeat. But the brave old hero replied that he had been sent there to try it on and would do so, or words to that effect.

"The forts had 115 guns of various kinds and sizes, mostly smooth-bore thirty-two-pounders. Above them lay the Confederate fleet of fifteen vessels, one of them an ironclad ram, another a large, unfinished floating battery covered with railroad iron. Two hundred Confederate sharpshooters kept constant watch along the riverbanks, and several fire-rafts were ready to be sent down among the Federal vessels. Both these and the sharpshooters were below the forts. Also there were two iron chains stretched across the river, supported upon eight hulks which were anchored abreast.

"Farragut's naval expedition was the largest that had ever sailed under the United States flag, consisting of six sloops of war, twenty-one mortar schooners, sixteen gunboats, and other vessels, carrying in all two hundred guns.

"But the vessels were built for the sea and were now to work in a much narrower space—a river with a shifting channel and obstructed by shoals.

"To get the larger vessels over the bar at the southwest pass was a work of time and great labor. They had to be made as light as possible and then dragged through a foot of mud. Two weeks of such labor was required to get the *Pensacola* over, and the *Colorado* could not be taken over at all.

"The mortar vessels were towed up stream and began to take their places. Porter disguised them with mud and the branches of trees, so that they could not be readily distinguished from the riverbanks, being moored under cover of the woods on the bank just below Fort Jackson. The stratagem was successful, and his vessels were moored where he wished to have them, the nearest being 2,850 yards from Fort Jackson, and 3,680 yards from Fort St. Philip.

"On the opposite side of the river, a little farther from the forts, Porter had his six remaining vessels stationed, screening them also with willows and reeds and mooring them under cover of the woods to conceal their true character.

"On the eighteenth of April, before nine o'clock in the morning, the attack was begun by a shot from Fort Jackson; then, as soon as Porter was ready, the *Owasco* opened fire, and the fourteen mortar boats concealed by the woods, also the six in full sight of the forts, began their bombardment.

"The gunboats took their part in the conflict by running up and firing heavy shells when the mortars needed relief. Porter was on the *Harriet Lane* in a position to see what was the effect of the shells and direct their aim accordingly.

"The fight went on for several days, then Farragut, deeming there was small prospect of reducing the forts, prepared to carry out another part of his instructions by running past them. He called a council of the captains in the cabin of the *Hartford*, and it was then and there decided that the attempt should be made.

"It was an intensely dark night, the wind blowing fiercely from the north, but Commander Bell with the *Winona*, the *Itasca*, *Kennebec*, *Iroquois*, and the *Pinola* ran up to the boom. The *Pinola* ran to the hulk under the guns of Fort Jackson, and an effort was made to destroy it with a petard, but failed. The *Itasca* was lashed to the next hulk, but a rocket sent up from the fort showed her to the foe, who immediately opened a heavy fire upon her. Half an hour of active work with chisels, saws, and sledges parted the boom of chains and logs, and the hulk to which she was attached swung around and grounded her in the mud in shallow water. But the *Pinola* rescued her.

"Two hours later an immense fire-raft came roaring down the stream, but it was caught by our men and rendered harmless. They would catch such things with grappling irons, tow them to the shore, and leave them there to burn out harmlessly.

"Day after day the bombardment went on, as fire-rafts came down the river every night, but Fort Jackson still held out, though its citadel had been set on fire by the shells from the mortar boats, and all the commissary stores and the clothing of the men destroyed.

The levee had been broken in scores of places by the exploding shells, so that the waters of the river flooded the parade ground and casemates.

"By sunset on the twenty-third, Farragut was ready for his forward movement, but Porter, with his mortar boats, was to stay and cover the advance with his fire. Farragut, onboard his flagship, the *Hartford*, was to lead the way with it, the *Brooklyn*, and the *Richmond*.

"These vessels formed the first division and were to keep near the right bank of the river, fighting Fort Jackson, while Captain Theodore Bailey was to keep close to the western bank with his— the second—division to fight Fort St. Philip. His vessels were the *Mississippi*, *Pensacola*, *Varuna*, *Oneida*, *Katahdin*, *Kineo*, *Wissahickon*, and the *Portsmouth*.

"Captain Bell still commanded the same vessels which I just mentioned as his, and his appointed duty was to attack the Confederate fleet above the forts, to keep the channel of the river, and push on, paying no attention to the forts themselves.

"In obedience to orders, the *Itasca* ran up to the boom, and at eleven o'clock showed a night signal that the channel was clear of obstruction excepting the hulks, which, with care, might be passed safely.

"A heavy fog and the settling of the smoke from the steamers upon the waters made the night a very dark one. No sound came from the forts, yet active preparations were going on in them for the approaching struggle, and their fleet was stationed near them in readiness to assist in the effort to prevent the Union vessels from ascending the river.

"At one o'clock every one on the Union ships was called to action, but the fleet remained stationary until two, and at half-past three Farragut's and Bailey's divisions were moving up the river, each on its appointed side, at the rate of four miles an hour.

"Then Porter's mortars, still at their moorings below the forts, opened upon those forts a terrible storm, sending as many as, if not more than, half a dozen shells with their fiery trails screaming through the air at the same moment.

"But no sound came from the forts until they discovered Captain Bailey's ship, the *Cayuga*, just as she had passed the boom, when they brought their heavy guns to bear upon her and broke the long silence with their roar.

"When she was close under Fort St. Philip she replied with heavy broadsides of grape and canisters as she passed on up the river.

"The other vessels of Bailey's division followed closely after, each imitating the *Cayuga's* example in delivering a broadside as she passed the forts, which they did almost unharmed with the exception of the *Portsmouth*, a sailing vessel, which lost her tow on firing her broadside and drifted down the river.

"Captain Bell and his division were not quite so fortunate. Three of his vessels passed the forts, but the *Itasca* received a storm of shot, one of which pierced her boiler. She drifted helplessly down the river. The *Kennebec* lost her way among the obstructions and went back to her moorings below. The *Winona*, too, recoiled from the storm.

"In the meantime, Farragut was in the fore rigging of the *Hartford*, watching with intense interest through his night glass the movements of the vessels under the command of Bailey and Bell, while the vessels he commanded in person were slowly nearing Fort Jackson. He was within a mile and a quarter of it when its heavy guns opened upon him. They were well aimed, and the *Hartford* was struck several times.

"Farragut replied with two guns that he had placed upon his forecastle, while at the same time he pushed on directly for the fort. When within a half mile of it he sheered off and gave them heavy broadsides of grape and canister—so heavy that they were driven from all their barbette guns. But the casemate guns were kept in full play, and the fight became a severe one.

"The *Richmond* soon joined in it, and the *Brooklyn* got entangled with some of the hulks that bore up the chain and so lagged behind. She had just succeeded in freeing herself from them when the Confederate ram *Manassas* came furiously down upon her. When she was within about ten feet, she fired a heavy bolt at the *Brooklyn* from her trap door, aiming for her smoke stack, but fortunately the shot lodged in some sandbags that protected her steam drum.

"The next moment the ram butted right into the *Brooklyn's* starboard gangway, but she was so effectually protected by chain armor that the *Manassas* glanced off, and then she disappeared in the darkness.

"All this time a raking fire from the fort had been pouring upon the *Brooklyn,* and just as she escaped from the *Manassas,* a large Confederate steamer attacked her. She pushed slowly on in the darkness, after giving the steamer a broadside that set it on fire and speedily destroyed it. She suddenly found herself abreast of Fort St. Philip.

"She was very close to it and speedily brought all her guns to bear upon it in a tremendous broadside.

"In his report Captain Craven said, 'I had the satisfaction of completely silencing that work before I left it, my men in the tops witnessing in the flashes of the shrapnel, the enemy running like sheep for more comfortable quarters.'

"While the *Brooklyn* was going through all this, Farragut was having what he called 'a rough time of it.' While he was battling with the forts, a huge fire-raft pushed by the *Manassas* came suddenly upon him all ablaze. In trying to avoid the fire-raft, the *Hartford* ran aground, and the incendiary came crashing alongside of her.

"In telling of it, Farragut said, 'In a moment the ship was one blaze all along the port side, halfway up the main and mizzen tops. But thanks to good organization of the fire department, by Lieutenant Thornton, the flames were extinguished, and at the same time we backed off and got clear of the raft. All this time we were pouring shells into the forts and they into us; now and then a rebel steamer would get under our fire and receive our salutation of a broadside.' The fleet had not fairly passed the forts when the Confederate ram and gunboats hastened to take part in the battle.

"The scene was now both grand and awful. Just think of 260 great guns and twenty mortars constantly firing, and shells exploding in and around the forts. It 'shook land and water like an earthquake,' Lossing tells us. 'And the surface of the river was strewn with dead and helpless fishes.' Major Bell, of Butler's staff, wrote of it, 'Combine all that you have ever heard of thunder, and add to it all you have ever seen of lightning, and you have, perhaps, a conception of the scene. And,' continues our historian, 'all this destructive energy, the blazing fire-rafts and floating volcanoes sending forth fire and smoke and bolts of death, the thundering forts, and the ponderous rams, were crowded, in the greatest darkness just before dawn, within the space of a narrow river. "Too narrow," said Farragut, "for more than two or three vessels to act to advantage. My greatest fear was that we should fire into each other; and Captain Wainwright and myself were hallooing ourselves hoarse at the men not to fire into our ships."'

"The *Cayuga* met the flotilla of Confederate rams and gunboats as soon as she passed Fort St. Philip. For a few minutes there were eighteen Confederate vessels intent upon her destruction."

"Was the *Manassas* one of the eighteen, sir?" queried Walter.

"Yes," replied the captain. "The floating battery *Louisiana* was another. Captain Mitchell was the name of her commander, and he was also the commandant of the remaining sixteen vessels of that rebel fleet.

"Captain Bailey could not fight so many at once without some assistance, so used his skill in avoiding the butting of the rams and the efforts to board his vessel. At the same time, he was making such good use of his guns that, while saving his own vessels, he compelled three of the Confederate gunboats to surrender to him before Captain Boggs and Lee, of the *Varuna* and the *Oneida,* came to his assistance.

"The *Cayuga* by that time had been struck forty-two times and was a good deal damaged in spars and rigging, but, in accordance with Farragut's orders, she moved up the river as the leader of the fleet.

"It was upon the *Varuna* that the enemy next poured out the vials of his wrath. In his report of the fight, Captain Boggs, her commander, said that immediately after passing the forts, he found himself 'amid a nest of rebel steamers.' He rushed into their midst, giving each a broadside as he passed. The first of those steamers seemed to be crowded with troops. One of the *Varuna's* shots exploded her boiler, and she drifted ashore. Next a gunboat and three other vessels were driven ashore in flames and presently blew up, one after another.

"Then the *Varuna* was furiously attacked by the *Governor Moore,* commanded by Beverly Kennon, one who had left the United States service for that of the rebels. His vessel raked along the *Varuna's* port, killing four men and wounding nine. Captain Boggs sent a three-inch shell into her, abaft her armor, and several shots from the after rifled gun, which partially disabled her, and she dropped out of action.

"In the meantime, another ram struck the *Varuna* under water with its iron prow, giving her a heavy blow in the port gangway. The *Varuna* answered with a shot, but it glanced harmlessly from the armored prow of the rebel ram. The ram, backing off a short distance, shot forward again, gave the *Varuna* another blow in the same place and crushed her side.

"But the ram had become entangled, and she was drawn around to the side of the *Varuna*, and Captain Boggs gave her five, eighteen shells abaft her armor from his port guns. In telling it afterward he said, 'This settled her and drove her ashore in flames.'

"But his own vessel was sinking. So he ran her into the bank, let go her anchor, and tied her bow up in the trees, all the time keeping his guns at work crippling the *Moore*.

"He did not cease firing till the water was over the gun tracks, but then he turned his attention to getting his wounded and the crew out of the vessel.

"Just then, Captain Lee, commander of the *Oneida*, came to his assistance. But Boggs waved him after the *Moore*, which was then in flames and presently surrendered to the *Oneida*. Kennon, her commander, had done a cowardly deed in setting her on fire and fleeing, leaving his wounded to the horrible fate of perishing in the flames. The surrender was, therefore, made by her second officer.

"That ended the fight on the Mississippi River. It had been a desperate one, but it lasted only an hour and a half, though nearly the whole of the rebel fleet was destroyed. The Federal loss was thirty killed and not more than 125 wounded."

Chapter Fourth

Captain Raymond paused, seemingly lost in thought. All waited in silence for a moment, then Violet, laying a hand on his arm, for she was seated close at his side, said with a loving smile into his eyes, "My dear, I fear we have been tiring you."

"Oh, no, not at all!" he replied, coming out of his reverie and taking possession of the pretty hand with a quiet air of ownership.

"I am sure nobody else is," said Walter. "So please go on, sir, won't you? And tell us all about the taking of the forest and the city."

"I will," replied the captain. "By the way, I want to tell you about a powder boy onboard the *Varuna,* Oscar Peck, a lad of only thirteen years, who showed coolness and bravery which would have entitled a man to praise.

"Captain Boggs was very much pleased with him, and in his report to Farragut praised him warmly. He said that seeing the lad pass quickly he asked where he was going in such a hurry. 'To get a passing box, sir,' replied the lad. 'The other was smashed by a ball.' When the *Varuna* went down Oscar disappeared. He had been standing by one of the guns and was thrown into the water by the movement of the vessel. But in a few minutes he was seen swimming toward the wreck. Captain Boggs was standing on a part of the ship that was still above water, when the lad climbed up by his side, gave the usual salute, and said, 'All right, sir, I report myself onboard.'"

"Ah," cried Walter exultantly, "he was a plucky American boy! I'm proud of him."

"Yes," said the captain, "and the more men and boys we have of a similar spirit the better for our dear land.

"But to go on with my story. Captain Bailey moved on up the river with his crippled vessel, the *Cayuga,* leaving the *Varuna* to continue the fight at the forts.

"A short distance above Fort St. Philip was the quarantine station. Opposite to it was a Confederate battery in charge of several companies of sharpshooters, commanded by Colonel Szymanski, a Pole.

"On perceiving the approach of the *Cayuga,* they tried to flee, but a volley of canister shot from her guns called a halt, and they were taken prisoners of war.

"By that time the battle at the forts was over and the remaining twelve ships presently joined the *Cayuga.* Then the dead were carried ashore and buried."

"Where was Butler all this time?" queried Walter.

"He had been busy preparing for his part of the work while the naval officers were doing theirs," was the reply. "His men were in transports at the passes and could hear distinctly the booming of the guns and mortars, but the general was at that time on the *Saxon,* which was following close in the rear of Bailey's division, until the plunging shot and shell into the water around her warned Butler that he had gone far enough. He then ordered the *Saxon* to drop a little astern, an order which was by no means disagreeable to her captain and was promptly obeyed, for he had onboard eight hundred barrels of gunpowder—a dangerous cargo, indeed, when exposed to the fiery missiles of the enemy."

"Wasn't it!" exclaimed Rosie.

"Where was Porter just then, sir?" asked Walter.

"He and his mortar fleet were still below the forts," replied the captain. "And just as Butler had ordered his vessel away from that dangerous spot, the rebel monitor *Manassas* came moving down into the midst of his fleet. She had just been terribly pounded by the *Mississippi* and was a helpless wreck, but that was not perceived at first. Some of the mortars opened fire upon her, but they stopped when they saw what was her condition. Her hull battered and pierced, her pipes twisted and riddled by shot, smoke pouring from every opening. In a few minutes her only gun went off, flames burst out from stern, trap door, and bow port, and she went hissing to the bottom of the river.

"Butler now hurried to his transports and took them to Sable Island, twelve miles in the rear of Fort St. Philip. From there they went in small boats, through the narrow and shallow bayous, piloted by Lieutenant Weitzel. It was a most fatiguing journey, the men sometimes having to drag their boats through cold, muddy water waist deep. But the brave, patriotic fellows worked on with a will, and by the night of the twenty-seventh they were at the quarantine, ready to begin the assault on Fort St. Philip the next day. They were landed under cover of the guns of the *Mississippi* and the *Kineo*. Butler sent a small force to the other side of the river above Fort Jackson, which Porter had been pounding terribly with the shells from his mortars. On the twenty-sixth, Porter sent a flag of truce with a demand to surrender of the fort, saying that Farragut had reached New Orleans and had taken possession.

"Colonel Higginson, the commander of the fort, replied that he had no official report of that surrender and that until he should receive such he would not surrender the fort. He could not entertain such a proposition for a moment.

"On the same day, General Duncan, commander of the coast defenses, but at that time in Fort Jackson, sent out an address to the soldiers, saying, 'The safety of New Orleans and the cause of the Southern Confederacy, our homes, our families, and everything dear to man yet depend upon our exertions. We are just as capable of repelling the enemy today as we were before the bombardment.'

"Thus he urged them to fight on. But they did not all agree with the views he expressed. They could see the blackened fragments of vessels and other property strewing the waters of the river as it flowed swiftly by, and the sight convinced them of the fall of New Orleans. They had heard, too, of the arrival of Butler's troops in the rear of Fort St. Philip.

"Doubtless they talked it over among themselves that night as a large number of them mutinied, spiked the guns bearing up the river, and the next day went out and surrendered themselves to Butler's pickets on that side of the river, saying they had been impressed and would not fight the government any longer. Their loss made the surrender of the fort a necessity, and Colonel Higginson accepted the generous terms offered him by Porter. He and Duncan went onboard the *Harriet Lane,* and the terms of surrender were reduced to writing.

"While that was going on in her cabin, a dastardly deed was done by the Confederate officer, Mitchell, who, as I have said, commanded the battery called the *Louisiana.* It lay above the forts. He had it towed out into the strong current, set her on fire, and abandoned her, leaving the guns all shotted, expecting she would float down and explode among Porter's mortar fleet. But a good Providence caused the explosion to come before she reached the fleet. It took place when she was abreast Fort St. Philip, and a soldier, one of its garrison, was killed by a flying fragment. Then she went to the bottom, and the rest of the Confederate steamers surrendered.

"Porter and his mortar fleet were still below the forts, but Farragut had now thirteen of his vessels safely above them and was ready to move on New Orleans.

"Half an hour after he reached the quarantine, he sent Captain Boggs to Butler with dispatches. Boggs went in a small boat through the shallow bayous in the rear of Fort St. Philip, and, as I have already said, the next day Butler and his troops arrived at the quarantine in readiness to assault the forts.

"Fort St. Philip was as perfect when taken by the Union forces as before the fight, and Fort Jackson was injured only in its interior works.

"The entire loss of the Federals in all this fighting was forty killed and 177 wounded. No reliable report was given of the Confederate losses in killed and wounded. The number of prisoners amounted to nearly one thousand.

"General Lovell, who had command of the Confederate troops at New Orleans, had gone down the river in his steamer *Doubloon* and arrived just as the Federal fleet was passing the forts. He was near being captured in the terrible fight that followed, but he escaped to the shore and hurried back to New Orleans as fast as courier horses could carry him.

"A rumor of the fight and its results had already reached the city, and when he confirmed it, a scene of wild excitement ensued. Soldiers hurried to and fro, women were in the street bareheaded, brandishing pistols and screaming, 'Burn the city! Never mind us! Burn the city!'

"Merchants fled from their stores, and military officers impressed vehicles to carry cotton to the levees to be burned. Four million dollars' worth of specie was sent out of the city by railway; foreigners crowded to the consulates to deposit money and other valuables for safety; and Twiggs, the traitor, fled, leaving to the care of a young woman the two swords that had been awarded him for his services in Mexico.

"Lovell believed that he had not a sufficient number of troops to defend the city and convinced the city authorities that such was the fact. He proceeded to disband the conscripts and to send munitions of war, stores of provisions, and other valuable property to the country by railroad and steamboats. Some of the white troops went to Camp Moore, seventy-eight miles distant by the railroad, but the Negro soldiers refused to go.

"The next morning Farragut came on up the river, meeting on the way blazing ships filled with cotton floating downstream. He presently discovered the Chalmette batteries on both sides of the river only a few miles below the city. The river was so full that the waters gave him complete command of those Confederate works. Causing his vessels to move in two lines, he set himself to the task of disabling them.

"Captain Bailey in the crippled *Cayuga* was pressing gallantly forward and did not notice the signal to the vessels to move in close order. He was so far ahead of the others that the fire of the enemy was for a time concentrated upon his vessel. For twenty minutes she sustained a heavy crossfire alone. But Farragut hastened forward with the *Hartford*, and, as he passed the *Cayuga*, he gave the batteries heavy broadsides of grape, shell, and shrapnel. So heavy were they that the first discharge drove the Confederates from their guns. The other vessels of the fleet followed the *Hartford's* example, and in twenty minutes the batteries were silenced, the men running for their lives.

"Oh, what a fearful scene our vessels passed through! The surface of the river was strewn with blazing cotton bales, burning steamers, and fire-rafts, all together sending up clouds of dense black smoke. But they were nearing the city, these Federal vessels, and the news that such was the case had caused another great panic. By order of the Governor of Louisiana and General Lovell, the destruction of property went on more rapidly than before. Great quantities of cotton, sugar, and other staple commodities of that region of the country were set on fire, so that for a distance of five miles there seemed to be a continuous sheet of flame accompanied by dense clouds of smoke. The people foolishly believed that the government, like themselves, regarded cotton as king, and that it was one of the chief objects for which the Federal troops were sent there. So they brought it in huge loads to the levee, piled it up there, and burned not less than fifteen hundred bales, worth about $1,500,000. For the same reason they burned more than a dozen large ships, some of which were loaded with cotton, as well as many magnificent steamboats, unfinished gunboats, and other vessels, sending them down the river wrapped in flames. They hoped that in addition to destroying the property the Federals were after, they might succeed in setting fire to and destroying their ships and boats.

"But the vessels of Farragut's squadron all escaped that danger, and in the afternoon, during a fierce thunderstorm, they anchored before the city.

"Captain Bailey was sent ashore with a flag and a summons from Farragut for the surrender of the city. He also demanded that the Confederate flag should be taken down from the public buildings and replaced with the Stars and Stripes.

"Escorted by sensible citizens, he made his way to the City Hall, through a cursing and hissing crowd. Lovell was still there and positively refused to surrender, but seeing that he was powerless to defend the city, he said so. Advising the mayor not to surrender or allow the flags to be taken down, he withdrew with his troops.

"The mayor was foolish enough to follow that advice and sent to Farragut a letter saying that though he and his people could not prevent the occupation of their city by the United States, they would not transfer their allegiance to that government, which they had already repudiated.

"While this was going on troops from the *Pensacola* had landed and hoisted the United States flag over the government mint, but scarcely had they retired from the spot, when the flag was torn down by some young men and dragged through the streets in dirision."

"Our flag! The glorious stripes and stars!" exclaimed Lulu, her eyes flashing. "I hope they didn't escape punishment for such an outrage as that?"

"One of them, a gambler, William B. Mumford by name, afterward paid the penalty for that and other crimes on the scaffold," replied her father. "A few hours after the pulling down of that flag, General Butler arrived and joined Farragut on the *Hartford*. On the twenty-ninth, Butler reported to the Secretary of War, and, referring to the treatment of the flag, said, 'This outrage will be punished in such a manner as in my judgment will caution both the perpetrators and the abettors of the act, so that they shall fear the stripes, if they do not reverence the stars, of our banner.'

"The secessionists expressed much exultation over the treatment of the flag and admiration of the rebellious deed.

"Farragut was very patient with the rebels, particularly the silly mayor—in reply to whose abusive letter he spoke of the insults and indignities to the flag and to his officers, adding, 'All of which go to show that the fire of this fleet may be drawn upon the city at any moment, and in such an event the levee would, in all probability, be cut by shells and an amount of distress ensue to the innocent population which I have heretofore endeavored to assure you that I desire by all means to avoid. The election therefore is with you; but it becomes me to notify you to remove the women and children from the city within forty-eight hours, if I have rightly understood your determination.'

"To this the foolish mayor sent a most absurd reply, saying that Farragut wanted to humble and disgrace the people and was talking nonsense about 'murdering women and children.' It was a decidedly insolent epistle, but the commander of a French ship of war that had just come in was still more impertinent. He wrote to Farragut that his government had sent him to protect the thirty thousand subjects in New Orleans and that he should demand sixty days, instead of forty-eight hours as the time to be given for the evacuation of the city. His letter closed with a threat: 'If it is your resolution to bombard this city, do it; but I wish to state that you will have to account for the barbarous act to the power which I represent.'

"Farragut was much perplexed and troubled with doubts as to what to do, but he was soon greatly relieved by the news of the surrender of the forts below, making it almost certain that Butler would soon be there to relieve him of the care of the city. With that prospect, he was able to quietly await the arrival of the land force.

"The people of New Orleans believed it impossible that those forts could be taken and deemed it safe to indulge in their defiant attitude toward the Federal forces already at their doors. But this unwelcome news convinced them of the folly and danger of further resistance and defiance of the general government, and a sort of apology was made to Farragut for the pulling down of the flag from the mint. It was said to have been the unauthorized act of men who performed it.

"The next day Captain Bell landed one hundred marines, hauled down the emblems of rebellion on the mint and Custom House, flung to the breeze the national flag in their places, then locking the Custom House door, carried the key to his vessel.

"There was a military organization in New Orleans called the European Brigade, which was composed of British, French, and Spanish aliens, whose ostensible purpose was to aid the authorities in protecting the citizens from unruly members. But now finding their occupation almost at an end, its English members voted at their armory that, as they would have no further use for their weapons and accoutrements, they should be sent to Beauregard's army at Corinth, as 'a slight token of their affection for the Confederate States.'"

"I should say that was a poor sort of neutrality," remarked Rosie.

"So I think," responded the captain. Then he went on with his story.

"Only a few hours after Mumford and his mates pulled down the flag, Butler arrived, joined Farragut on the *Hartford,* and presently made to the Secretary of War the report of which I have already spoken.

"He hurried back to his troops and made quick arrangements for their immediate advance up the river. On the first of May he appeared before New Orleans with his transports bearing two thousand men. The general and his wife, his staff, and fourteen hundred troops were on the *Mississippi*—the vessel in which he had sailed from Hampton Roads sixty-five days before.

"At four o'clock on the afternoon of that day the troops began to land. First came a company of the Thirty-first Massachusetts, presently followed by the rest of the regiment, the Fourth Wisconsin, and Everett's battery of heavy field guns.

"They formed in procession, acting as an escort to General Butler and General Williams and his staff, and marched through several streets to the Custom House, their band playing the "Star-Spangled Banner." They had been given strict directions not to resent any insults that might be offered by the vast crowd gathered in the streets, unless ordered so to do. If a shot should be fired from any house, they were to halt, arrest the inmates, and destroy the building.

"Their patience was greatly tried during that short march, the crowd constantly growing greater and more boisterous and pouring out upon them volleys of abusive epithets, both vulgar and profane, applying them to the general as well as his troops."

"I think anybody but an American would have ordered his soldiers to fire upon them for that," remarked Walter. "Did they do no fighting at all at the time, sir?"

"No," replied the captain. "They were obedient to the orders of their superior officers and brave enough to endure the undeserved abuse in silence.

"At length their final destination was reached, Captain Everett posted his cannon around the Custom House, quarters there were given to the Massachusetts regiment, and the city remained comparatively quiet through the night.

"General Butler passed the night onboard the *Mississippi*, and at an early hour in the evening sent out a proclamation to the citizens of New Orleans. It was first sent to the office of the *True Delta* to be printed, but the proprietor flatly refused to use his type in such an act of submission to Federal rule."

"I hope he wasn't allowed to do as he pleased about it?" growled Walter.

"I think hardly," returned the captain with an amused smile. "Some two hours later a file of soldiers were in his office, half a dozen of whom were printers, and in a very short time the proclamation was sent out in printed form.

"Meanwhile the Federal officers had taken their possession of city quarters. General Butler was at the St. Charles Hotel and invited the city authorities to a conference with him there. Mayor Monroe told the messenger sent to him that his place of business was at City Hall. He was answered by a suggestion that such a reply was not likely to prove satisfying to the commanding general. He then prudently decided to go and wait on General Butler at the St. Charles.

"Some of his friends accompanied him, among them Pierre Soule, who had been a representative to Congress before the war.

"General Butler and these callers had a talk together in regard to the proper relations existing between the general government and the city of New Orleans, Butler maintaining that the authority of the government of the United States was and ought to be supreme. He went on to state that it had a right to demand the allegiance of the people and that no other authority could be allowed to conflict with it in ruling the city.

"The mayor, Soule, and his friends, on the contrary, insisted that Louisiana was an independent sovereignty and to her alone the people owed their allegiance. They asserted that the national troops were invaders, the people were doing right in treating them with contempt and abhorrence, and that they would be fully justified in driving them away if it were in their power to do so.

"While this heated discussion was going on, a messenger came from General Williams, who had command of the regiment protecting headquarters, saying that he feared he could not control the mob which had collected in the street.

"Butler calmly replied: 'Give my compliments to General Williams, and tell him if he finds he cannot control the mob, to open upon them with artillery.'

"At that the mayor and his friends sprang to their feet, exclaiming excitedly, 'Don't do that, General.' Butler asked, 'Why not?' and went on, 'The mob must be controlled. We can't have a disturbance in the street.'

"At that the mayor stepped out upon the balcony and spoke to the mob, telling them of the general's orders and advising them to disperse.

"At that interview General Butler read to his callers the proclamation he was about to issue. Soule told him it would give great offense, and that the people would never submit to its demands, for they were not conquered and could not be expected to act as a conquered people would. 'Withdraw your troops and leave the city government to manage its own affairs,' he said. 'If the troops remain there will certainly be trouble.'"

"And Butler, of course, did as he was told," laughed Rosie.

"Not exactly," returned the captain. "'I did not expect to hear from Mr. Soule a threat on this occasion,' he said. 'I have long been accustomed to hear threats from Southern gentlemen in political conventions, but let me assure the gentlemen present that the time for tactics of that nature has passed, never to return. New Orleans is a conquered city. If not, why are we here? Have you opened your arms and bid us welcome? Are we here by your consent? Would you, or would you not expel us if you could? New Orleans has been conquered by the forces of the United States, and by the laws of all nations lies subject to the will of the conquerors.'"

"Some of the New Orleans people, especially the women, behaved very badly, did they not, captain?" asked Evelyn.

"Yes, though no maid was injured by the troops, who behaved in a perfectly orderly manner. No woman was treated with the slightest disrespect, though the women were very offensive in their manifestations of contempt of the officers, not omitting even the commanding officer himself. They would leave street cars and church pews when a Federal officer entered them. They would leave the sidewalks also, going around the gentlemen and turning up their noses and sometimes uttering abusive words. They wore secession colors in their bonnets, sang rebel songs, and turned their backs on passing soldiers. When out on their balconies, they played airs that were used with rebel words. Indeed, they tried to show in every possible way their contempt and aversion for the Union officers and soldiers. At length a woman of the 'dominant class,' meeting two Union officers on the street, spit in their faces. Then General Butler decided to at once put a stop to such proceedings, and on the fifth of May he issued order number twenty-eight, which had the desired effect."

"What was the order, papa? What did he order the people or the soldiers to do?" queried Lulu.

"The amount of the order was that every woman who should behave as that one had, insulting or showing contempt for any officer or soldier of the United States, should be regarded and held liable to be treated as not of good moral character. The mayor made it the subject of another impudent letter to General Butler, for which he was arrested. But he was soon released again upon making a humble apology."

"Did they let him remain mayor of the city, papa?" asked Gracie.

"No. Instead, General G. F. Sheply of Maine was appointed Military Governor of New Orleans, and he made an excellent one, having the city made cleaner and, in consequence, more wholesome than it had been for years, if ever before. Soon after that William B. Mumford was arrested, tried by a military court for treason in having torn down the flag, found guilty, and hanged."

Chapter Fifth

*T*here was a moment of silence broken by Lulu with an eager exclamation. "Oh, papa, don't you remember that when we were at Saratoga last summer you promised that some time you would tell us about the fighting in the Revolution near and at Fort Schuyler? Won't you please do it now?"

"I will if the others wish to hear it," he replied, and a general eager assent being given, he at once began the story.

"Fort Schuyler," he said, "at first called Fort Stanwix in honor of the general of that name, who directed the work of its erection, stood at the head of boat navigation on the Mohawk, where the village of Rome now is. It cost the British and Colonial government $266,400 and was a strong post of resistance from any attack of the French in Canada with whom, as you all know, I think, the colonists were often at war on their own account or that of the mother country. It commanded the portage between Lake Ontario and the Mohawk Valley and was the theater of many stirring events during the War of the Revolution. Indians and Tories terrorized the people who lived there and who were loyal to the cause of their country. There were daylight struggles and stealthy midnight attacks in such numbers that Tryon County came to be spoken of as 'the dark and bloody ground.'

"Congress, perceiving the importance of defending the northern and western frontiers of New York from incursions by the British and Indians, sent General Schuyler to strengthen old Fort Stanwix, which had been allowed to fall into a state of decay so that it was little more than a ruin, and, if he found it necessary, to erect other fortifications.

"General Phillip Schuyler was a gentleman of fortune, of military skill, experience, sound judgment, and lofty patriotism. Lossing tells us that, 'for causes quite inexplicable, he was superseded in effect by Gates in March of 1777, only to be reinstated in May. No appointment could have been more acceptable to the people of northern New York, who were at that time in a state of great excitement and alarm.'

"In recent campaigns against the French and Indians of Lakes Champlain and George, General Schuyler had done great service to the colony and the people along the northern frontier. That of itself was sufficient cause for attachment to him, besides his many virtues which had endeared him to all who knew him. In fighting the British he would be defending his own home and large landed estate.

"In March of 1777, Burgoyne arrived in Quebec, bearing the commission of lieutenant-general, and by the first of June, a force of seven thousand men was collected for him and mustered at St. John's at the foot of Lake Champlain. Also the British Lieutenant-colonel St. Leger was sent with a force of seven hundred rangers up the St. Lawrence and Lake Ontario to Oswego. He was to gather the Indians, make friends with them, and get them to act as his allies. Then he was to sweep the valley of the Mohawk with help of Johnson and his Tories, take Fort Schuyler, and afterward join Burgoyne.

"Colonel Peter Gausevoort was at that time in command of Fort Schuyler. The people of Tryon County, hearing of St. Leger's movement and that a descent was to be made upon them by the way of Oswego, were greatly alarmed. In June, a man from Canada was arrested as a spy, and from him the Americans learned that a detachment of British, Canadians, and Indians was coming against them on their way to join Burgoyne at Albany."

"But Burgoyne never got there—to Albany—until he went as a prisoner. Did he, sir?" asked Walter.

"No, my boy, he was defeated and made prisoner while on his way to the city. The Battle of Saratoga was a disastrous one to the invaders of our land.

"The intelligence of which I just spoke as given by the spy was afterward confirmed by Thomas Spencer, a friendly Oneida sachem, who was sent to Canada as a secret emissary and there became acquainted with the plans of Burgoyne.

"For a time the loyal people, the Whigs, who were for their native land and not for the English king, who had been showing himself a tyrant and oppressor, were almost paralyzed with alarm. Fort Schuyler was still unfinished and the garrison feeble. But Colonel Gansevoort was hopeful, vigilant, and active. He wrote urgently to General Schuyler for aid, and the general made a like appeal to the Provincial Congress of New York and the general Congress. But it was too late for them to send him help before the attack would be made.

"On the second of August, Brant and Lieutenant Bird began the investment of the fort, and on that very day Gansevoort and his little garrison of 750 men received a reinforcement of two hundred men under Lieutenant-colonel Melon, and two bateaux loaded with provisions and military stores—a most welcome addition to the scant supplies in the fort.

"The next day Colonel St. Leger arrived with the rest of his troops. The siege was begun on the fourth. The Indians, hiding in the bushes, wounded some of our men who were at work on the parapets, and a few bombs were thrown into the fort.

"The next day it was the same. The Indians spread themselves about through the woods encircling the fort, and all through the night they tried to intimidate the Americans by their hideous yells.

"On that very day General Herkimer was coming to their aid with more than eight hundred men of the militia of Tryon County. He was near Oriskany, a little village eight miles east of the fort. From there he sent a messenger to tell Colonel Gansevoort that he was approaching and asked to be informed of that messenger's arrival by the firing of three guns in quick succession, knowing that they could be heard in Oriskany. Unfortunately, his messenger did not reach the fort until the next day, and Herkimer, who though brave was cautious, decided to halt till he should hear the signal or receive reinforcements. Some of his officers and men were impatient to push on.

"Herkimer would not consent, and two of his colonels, Paris and Cox, called him a coward and a Tory. Herkimer replied calmly, 'I am placed over you as a father and guardian and shall not lead you into difficulties from which I may not be able to extricate you.'

"They continued their taunts and demands till he was stung into giving the command, 'March on!'

"St. Leger knew of the advance of Herkimer and his troops and sent a division of Johnston's Greens, under Major Watts, Brant with a strong body of Indians, and Colonel Butler with his rangers to intercept him and prevent his making an attack upon the entrenchments which he had made about Fort Schuyler.

"Gansevoort noticed the silence in the enemy's camp and also the movement of his troops down toward the river along the margin of the wood. When the courier came with the message from Herkimer he understood the meaning of it all, and immediately fired the signal guns.

"Herkimer had said in his message that he intended, on hearing the signals, to cut his way through the camp of the enemy to the fort and asked that a sortie from it should be made at the same time.

"As quickly as possible Gansevoort had it made. A detachment of two hundred men of his own and Wesson's regiments with an iron three-pounder were detailed for the duty. Then fifty more were added for the protection of the cannon and to assist in whatever way they could. Colonel Marinus Willett was given the command.

"It was raining heavily while all of the necessary preparations were going on in the fort, but the moment it ceased, Willett had his men hastened out to attack the enemy furiously.

"The advanced guard was driven in, and so sudden and impetuous was the charge that Sir John Johnson had no time to put on his coat. He tried to bring his troops into order, but they were so panic-stricken that they fled, and he with them. They crossed the river to St. Leger's camp, and the Indians concealed themselves well in the deep forest.

"The Americans took much plunder—all Sir Johnson's baggage and his papers, as well as those of other officers, giving valuable information to the garrison of Fort Schuyler and the British colors, of which there were five. The Americans presently raised it upon their flagstaff beneath their own rude flag. It had been fashioned, as I have already told some of you, out of strips of red and white obtained by tearing up men's shirts for the one, and joining bits of scarlet cloth for the other, while a blue cloak that belonged to Captain Abraham Swartwout of Duchess County, then in the fort, was used to form the ground for the white stars. The staff upon which all these hung was in full view of the enemy. Then the whole garrison mounted the parapets and made the forest ring with three loud cheers.

"While all this was going on in and around the fort, General Herkimer and his men were coming toward it through the woods. It was a dark, sultry morning. The troops were chiefly militia regiments and marched in an irregular, careless way, neglecting proper precautions.

"Brant and his Tories took good advantage of this carelessness, hid themselves in a ravine which crossed Herkimer's path and had a thick growth of underwood along its margin, which made it easy for them to conceal themselves. When all except the rear guard of the unsuspecting Americans had entered the ravine, where the ground was marshy and crossed by a causeway of earth and logs, Brant gave a sign, immediately followed by a warhoop, and the Indians fell upon our poor men with spear, hatchet, and rifle ball. As Lossing says, 'like hail from the clouds that hovered over them.'

"The rear guard fled and left the others to their fate, yet perhaps they suffered more from the pursuing Indians than they would if they had stood their ground, helping their fellows. The attack had been so sudden that there was great confusion in the ranks, but they presently recovered, fought like veterans, and fought bravely for their lives and for their country."

"Were many of them killed, sir?" asked Walter.

"Yes," replied the captain sighing. "The slaughter was dreadful, and the good general was soon among the wounded. A musket ball passed through his horse, killing it and sadly wounding him, shattering his leg just below the knee. He at once ordered the saddle taken from his horse and placed against a large beech tree near by, and there he sat during the rest of the fight, calmly giving his orders while the enemy's bullets whistled around him like sleet, killing and wounding his men on every side."

"He was no coward, after all," exclaimed Walter, his eyes shining. "But did any of our men escape being killed, sir?"

"After a little they formed themselves into circles," continued the captain, "so meeting the enemy at all points. Their fire became so destructive that the Tories and the Johnson Greens charged with the bayonet, and the patriots being equally prompted to defend themselves, it became a terrible hand-to-hand fight.

"It was at length stopped by the shower that had delayed the sortie from the fort—both parties seeking shelter under the trees. Then, as soon as the shower was over, Colonel Willett made his sally from the fort, attacking Johnson's camp, and the battle at Oriskany was renewed.

"It is said to have been the bloodiest of the war in proportion to the numbers engaged. It is stated that about one-third of the militia fell on the battleground and as many more were mortally wounded or carried into captivity. About fifty wounded were carried from the field on litters, General Herkimer among them. He was taken to his own home where he died ten days afterward."

"But who gained the victory, papa?" asked Lulu.

"The Americans, the others having fled, but they were unable to accomplish the object of the expedition—the relief of Fort Schuyler. Surrounded by the enemy, the men in the fort could gain no intelligence as to the results of the fight at Oriskany, and St. Leger took advantage of their ignorance to falsely represent the British to have been the victors to the total defeat of the Americans and announce a victorious advance by Burgoyne.

"Two American officers, Colonel Billenger and Major Frey, who had been taken prisoners, were forced to write a letter to Colonel Gansevoort, containing many misrepresentations and advising him to surrender. This Colonel Butler delivered to Gansevoort and verbally demanded his surrender.

"Gansevoort refused, saying he would not answer such a summons verbally made unless by St. Leger himself.

"The next morning Butler and two other officers drew near the fort carrying a white flag and asked to be admitted as bearers of a message to the commander of the fort.

"The request was granted, but they were first blindfolded before they were conducted to the dining room of the fort, where they were received by Gansevoort. The windows of the room closed and candles lighted."

"What was that for, papa?" asked Gracie.

"To prevent them from seeing what was the condition of things within the fort," replied her father.

"And was Gansevoort alone with them, papa?"

"No. He had with him Colonels Willett and Mellon. Butler and his companions were politely received, and one of them, Major Aneram by name, made a little speech, telling of the humanity of St. Leger's feelings and his desire to prevent bloodshed. They said that St. Leger found it difficult to keep the Indians in check, and the only salvation of the garrison was an immediate surrender of the fort and all of its stores. Officers and soldiers would be allowed to keep their baggage and other private property, and their personal safety would be guaranteed. He added that he hoped these honorable terms would be immediately accepted, for if not it would not be in St. Leger's power to offer them again."

"So the Americans, of course, were afraid to reject them?" sniffed Walter.

"Hardly," returned the captain with a smile. "But that was not all Aneram said with a view of inducing them to do so. He went on to say that the Indians were eager to march down the country, laying waste and killing inhabitants, that Herkimer's relief corps had been totally destroyed, Burgoyne had possession of Albany, and there was no longer any hope for this garrison."

"What a liar he was, that Aneram!" exclaimed Walter. "Why Burgoyne had not even got so far as Saratoga then."

"No," responded the captain. "And the bright and plucky officers of Fort Schuyler, to whom he was speaking, were not so easily hoodwinked. They saw through his designs and were not to be deceived by the falsehoods and misrepresentations of his address.

"It was Colonel Willett who, with the approval of Gansevoort, made answer, speaking, as Lossing says, with 'emphasis,' and looking Aneram full in the face.

"'Do I understand you, sir? I think you say that you came from a British colonel, who is commander of the army that invests this fort; and, by your uniform, you appear to be an officer in the British service. You have made a long speech on the occasion of your visit, which, stripped of all its superfluities, amounts to this: that you come from a British colonel to the commandant of this garrison, to tell him that, if he does not deliver up the garrison into the hands of your colonel, he will send his Indians to murder our women and children. You will please reflect, sir, that their blood will be upon your heads, not upon ours. We are doing our duty; this garrison is committed to our care, and we will take care of it. After you get out of it, you may turn round and look at its outside, but never expect to come in again unless you come as a prisoner. I consider the message you have brought a degrading one for a British officer to send, and by no means reputable for a British officer to carry. For my own part, I declare, before I would consent to deliver this garrison to such a murdering set as your army, by your own account, consists of, I would suffer my body to be filled with splinters and set on fire, as you know has at times been practiced by such hordes of women and children killers as belong to your army.'"

"Good!" said Walter. "And the other two American officers, I suppose, agreed with him."

"Yes," Captain Raymond replied. "And they all felt satisfied that they would not be so urgently pressed to surrender at once, and on conditions so favorable, if their prospects were as dark as their besiegers would have them believe."

Chapter Sixth

"St. Leger made another effort to induce them so do so," continued Captain Raymond. "On the ninth he sent a written demand offering about the same terms as before.

"Gansevoort replied in writing: 'Sir, your letter of this date I have received, in answer to which I say, that it is my determined resolution, with the force under my command, to defend this fort to the last extremity, in behalf of the United States, who have placed me here to defend it against all their enemies.'"

"Did the British give it up then?" asked Gracie.

"No. They began to dig and make preparations to run a mine under the strongest bastion of the fort, while at the same time they sent out an address to the people of Tryon County, signed by Clause, Johnson, and Butler, urging them to submit to British rule, asserting that they themselves were desirous to have peace, and threatening that in case of refusal all the horrors of Indian cruelty would be visited upon them. Also they called upon the principal men of the valley to come up to Fort Schuyler and compel its garrison to surrender, as they would be forced to do in the end."

"Did the men in the fort give up then, papa?" queried Gracie.

"No, no, indeed, little daughter!" he replied. "They were brave men and staunch patriots, and they had no intention to surrender so long as they could possibly hold out. Fearing ammunition might give out and their supply of provisions, too, they resolved to send word to General Schuyler, who was then at Stillwater, asking for aid from him in their sore extremity.

"Of course it would be a hazardous attempt, but Colonel Willett offered to be the messenger. One stormy night, he and Lieutenant Stockwell left the fort at ten o'clock by the sallyport, each armed with a spear, and crept along the morass on hands and knees to the river, which they crossed upon a log. Their way lay through a tangled wood, and they soon lost it. The bark of a dog presently warned them that they were near an Indian camp, and fearing to either advance or retreat they stood still there for several hours.

"But at length the dawn of day showed them where they were, so that they were able to find the right road and pursue their way. They took a zigzag course, now on land, now through the bed of a stream, to foil any attempt on the part of some possible pursuer to gain upon them by the scent of their footsteps.

"They arrived safely at the German Flats, mounted fleet horses, and sped down the valley to the quarters of General Schuyler. On arriving, they learned that he had already heard of the defeat of Herkimer and was preparing to send succor to the besieged in the fort.

"Meanwhile St. Leger was pressing his siege, and the garrison, hearing nothing of the successful journey of their messengers or of aid coming to them from any quarter, began to grow despondent and to hint to their commander that it might be best to surrender, as their supply of both provisions and ammunition was getting low.

"But Gansevoort was too brave and hopeful to think of so doing. He told the despondent ones that in case help did not arrive before their supplies were exhausted, they would sally forth in the night and cut their way through the enemy's camp.

"But relief came in an unexpected manner that always reminds me of that siege of Samaria by the host of the Syrians in the days of Elisha the prophet of Israel. The way the Lord took to deliver them, causing 'the Syrians to hear a noise of chariots and a noise of horses, even the noise of a great host, and they said one to another, "Lo, the king of Israel hath hired against us the kings of the Hittites and the kings of the Egyptians to come upon us." Wherefore they arose and fled in the twilight, and left their tents and their horses, and their asses, even the camp as it was, and fled for their lives.' For suddenly and mysteriously the British, Indians, and Tories besieging Fort Schuyler did the same—they fled, leaving tents, artillery, and camp equipage behind them."

"Why, papa, how very strange!" exclaimed Lulu. "Were they frightened in the same way?"

"Not exactly the same but somewhat like it," replied her father. "General Schuyler, at the mouth of the Mohawk, made an appeal to his men for volunteers to go to the relief of Gansevoort, now besieged by the enemy in Fort Schuyler. Arnold and his troops, most of them Massachusetts men, responded with alacrity and, joined by the First New York regiment, they marched at once.

"Arnold's force was much smaller than that of St. Leger's, and he resorted to strategem as the only means of securing his end. A nephew of General Herkimer, named Hon-Yost Schuyler, who was a coarse, ignorant fellow, had been taken prisoner along with Walter Butler. You remember, the one who had been arrested while carrying to the people of Tryon County the call for them to force the defenders of Fort Schuyler to surrender, and was tried and condemned as a spy.

"The same thing had befallen Hon-Yost, but his mother pleaded for him, and though at first Arnold was inexorable, he at length agreed to release the fellow on condition that he would go to Fort Schuyler and alarm St. Leger with the story that the Americans were coming against him in force to compel the raising of the siege.

"Hon-Yost managed the business with great adroitness. Before leaving he had seven bullets shot through his coat, which he showed to the British and Indians on arriving at their encampment as proof of 'a terrible engagement with the enemy.' He was acquainted with many of the Indians, and when he came rushing into the camp almost out of breath with haste and apparent fright, telling this story with the added information that the Americans were coming and that he had barely escaped with his life, his hearers were very much alarmed.

"They asked what were the numbers of the Americans, and in reply he shook his head mysteriously, pointing as he did so to the leaves on the trees, as if he would say that they were numberless.

"The Indians, who had been uneasy and moody since the Battle of Oriskany, and were at the moment of Hon-Yost's arrival holding a pow-wow to plead with the 'Great Spirit' to guide and direct them, at once resolved to flee and told St. Leger of their decision.

"He sent for Hon-Yost, questioned him, and was told that Arnold would be there in twenty-four hours with two thousand men.

"Hon-Yost had come in to the camp alone, he and the Oneida chief having laid their plans beforehand. The chief was to arrive a little later than the other, so that they would not appear to be in collusion, and just as Hon-Yost finished his story to St. Leger, the chief and two or three straggling Indians of his tribe, who had joined him on his way, came in with the same story of the near approach of a large body of Americans. One told St. Leger that Arnold had three thousand men with him and another that the army of Burgoyne was cut to pieces. They pretended that a bird had brought them news that the valley below was swarming with warriors.

"The savages were now thoroughly alarmed, and all the bribes and promises of St. Leger could not induce them to remain any longer. They suspected foul play and would not touch the strong drink he offered. When, finding that they would go, he asked them to take the rear in retreating, they indignantly refused, saying, 'You mean to sacrifice us. When you marched down you said there would be no fighting for Indians, we might go down and smoke our pipes; numbers of our warriors have been killed, and you mean to sacrifice us also.'

"The council broke up, the Indians fled, the panic was communicated to the rest of the army, and they fled in terror to their boats on Oneida Lake. The Indians made merry of their flight, hurrying on after them with the warning cry: 'They are coming! They are coming!' So alarmed were the Tories and British troops that they threw away their knapsacks and their arms as they ran. Also the Indians killed or robbed many of them and took their boats, so that St. Leger said, 'they became more formidable than the enemy we had to expect.'"

"And did the Americans chase them that time, sir?" asked Walter.

"Yes. Gansevoort at once sent word to Arnold that the British were retreating, and Arnold sent nine hundred men in pursuit. The next day he himself had reached the fort, but he and his men presently marched back to the main army, then at Stillwater, leaving Colonel Willett in command of Fort Schuyler.

"So ended the siege of which Lossing says that 'in its progress were shown the courage, skill, and endurance of the Americans everywhere so remarkable in the revolution.'"

"Yes, sir," said Walter. "But will you please tell what became of Hon-Yost?"

"Yes. He went with the British as far as Wood Creek, then managed to desert and at once carried the news of Arnold's approach to Fort Schuyler. He went back to Fort Dayton, afterward fled with his family and fourteen of his Tory friends, and joined Sir John Johnson. When the war was over, he returned to the valley where he died in 1818."

Chapter Seventh

"*N*ow, papa, if you're not too tired won't you please tell us about the writing of the 'Star-Spangled Banner'?" pleaded Lulu with a smiling, coaxing look up into her father's face.

"I am not too tired, and if all wish to hear it, will willingly tell the story to the best of my ability," he replied, taking in his and softly patting the hand she had laid on his knee.

"I'm sure we will all be glad to hear it, sir," said Walter. "It happened in the War of 1812, didn't it?"

"Yes. The British had taken Washington, where they had behaved more like vandals than civilized men, burning and destroying both public buildings and private property—the Capitol, the President's house, the Arsenal, the Library of Congress, and barracks for three thousand troops. Besides that private property—a large ropewalk, some houses on Capitol Hill, and a tavern—all of which they burned. The light of the fire was seen at Baltimore, and the news of the capture of Washington caused intense excitement there— particularly because it was known that the British were quite exasperated at the Baltimoreans on account of its being the place whence had been sent out many a swift clipper—from whence built vessels and expert seamen had struck heavy blows at British commerce on the high seas.

"Baltimore is on the Patapsco River, ten miles from the Chesapeake Bay. The narrow strait connecting harbor and bay is defended by Fort McHenry, which stood there at that time. It was expected that Baltimore would be the next point of attack by the enemy, and there was, of course, great excitement.

"General Samuel Smith, who had been a Revolutionary officer, at once exerted himself to prepare both Baltimore and Annapolis for successful defense. He was a fine officer. You all perhaps remember him as commander at Fort Mifflin when attacked by the British and Hessians in the Revolutionary War. He had been active in this war also, ever since the appearance of the British squadron in the Chesapeake during the spring of the previous year of 1813."

"And this was in the fall of 1814, was it not, captain?" queried Evelyn.

"Yes, in early September. In the spring of 1813, it was rumored that the British were coming to attack the city, and several persons were arrested as traitors and spies. Also, five thousand men were quickly called to arms ready to defend the city, and companies of militia came pouring in from the country. All this within a few hours.

"Then General Striker's brigade and some other military bodies, to the number of five thousand with four pieces of artillery, were reviewed. The marine artillery of Baltimore was 160 in number, commanded by Captain George Stiles, and composed of masters and masters' mates of vessels there. It was a corps celebrated for its gallantry, and it was warmed with forty-two-pounders.

"Finding the city so well prepared to give them a warm reception, the British abandoned their intention to attack it, went to sea, and

Baltimore enjoyed a season of repose. But, as I have been telling you, they returned after the capture of Washington, and again the people set to work at preparations for the city's defense.

"General Smith was made first in command of all the military force intended to insure the safety of the city. But it is with the attack upon Fort McHenry and its repulse that we are concerned. The fort was garrisoned by about a thousand men under the command of Major George Armistead."

"Regulars, sir?" asked Walter.

"Some were, others volunteers," replied the captain. "There were, besides, four land batteries to assist in the work. But I will not go into particulars in regard to them, as I know they would be rather uninteresting to the greater part of my listeners.

"It was on Sunday evening, September eleventh, that the British were seen in strong force at the mouth of the Patapsco, preparing to land at North Point, which lay fifteen miles from the city by land, twelve by water. Their fleet anchored off that point, two miles from the shore. It was a beautiful night, a full moon shining in a cloudless sky, and the air was balmy.

"Ross intended to take Baltimore by surprise, and he had boasted that he would eat Sunday dinner there. At two o'clock in the morning the boats were lowered from his ships, and seamen and land troops went on shore, protected by several gun brigs anchored very near. The men were armed, of course, and each boat had a carronade ready for action. Admiral Cockburn and General Ross were on shore by about seven o'clock with five thousand land troops, two thousand seamen, and two thousand marines.

"Their intention was to march rapidly upon Baltimore and take it by surprise, therefore, they carried as little baggage as possible, and only eighty rounds apiece of ammunition. At the same time a frigate was sent to make soundings in the channel leading to Baltimore, as the navy was intended to take part in the attack upon the city."

"Wasn't everybody terribly frightened, papa?" asked Gracie.

"There was a good deal of alarm," replied the captain. "Many of the citizens fled with their valuables to places in the interior of the country, filling the hotels for nearly a hundred miles north of the city.

"I will not at present go into the details of the Battle of North Point, which immediately followed, but will tell of what was going on upon the water.

"The British frigate, schooners, sloops, and bomb ketches had passed into the Patapsco early in the morning, while Ross was moving from North Point, and anchored off Fort McHenry, beyond the reach of its guns. The bomb and rocket vessels were so posted as to act upon Fort McHenry and the fortifications on the hill commanded by Rodgers. The frigates were stationed farther outward, as the water was too shallow to allow them to approach within four or five miles of the city, or two and a half of the fort.

"Besides, the Americans had sunk twenty-four vessels in the narrow channel between Fort McHenry and Lazaretto Point to prevent the passage of the vessels of the enemy.

"That night was spent by the British fleet in preparations for the morrow's attack upon the fort and the entrenchments on the hill. On the morning of the thirteenth their bomb vessels opened a heavy fire upon the American works, at about seven o'clock and at a distance of two miles. They kept up a heavy bombardment until three o'clock in the afternoon.

"Armistead at once opened the batteries of Fort McHenry upon them, but, after keeping up a brisk fire for some time, discovered that his missiles fell short and were harmless. It was a great disappointment to find that he must endure the tremendous shower of the shells of the enemy without being able to return it in kind, or do anything whatever to check it. But our brave fellows kept at their posts, enduring the storm with great courage and fortitude.

"At length a bombshell dismounted one of the twenty-four-pounders, killing Lieutenant Claggett and wounding several of his men. That caused some confusion, which Cockrane perceived, and hoping to profit by it, he ordered three of his bomb vessels to move up nearer the fort, thinking to thus increase the effectiveness of his guns.

"No movement could have been more acceptable to Armistead, and he quickly took advantage of it, ordering a general cannonade and bombardment from every part of the fort, thus punishing the enemy so severely that in less than half an hour he fell back to his old anchorage.

"One of their rocket vessels was so badly injured that, to save her from being entirely destroyed, a number of small boats had to be sent to tow her out of the reach of Armistead's guns. The garrison gave three cheers and ceased firing.

"The British vessels returned to their former stations and again opened fire, keeping up with little intermission a furious bombardment until past midnight, when it was discovered that the British had sent a pretty large force up the Patapsco to capture Fort Covington, then attack Fort McHenry in the rear. For this purpose there had been sent 1,250 men in barges with scaling ladders and other implements for storming the fort. But providentially their errand was made known to the garrison of Fort McHenry in good season by the throwing up of rockets to examine the shores. Not only the fort but also two redoubts on the Patapsco immediately opened a heavy fire upon them and drove them away.

"So heavy was the firing that the houses of Baltimore were shaken to their very foundations. Lossing tells us that Rodger's men in Fort Covington worked their guns with effect, but Webster's continuous cannonade with his six-gun battery provided the final repulse of the enemy. The historian adds that he thinks it not too much to say that Webster's gallant conduct on that occasion saved both Fort McHenry and the city."

"Were any of the British killed?" asked Walter.

"Yes, quite a few, and two of their vessels sunk."

"And did they go on firing at the fort?"

"They did, until seven o'clock in the morning of the fourteenth, then ceased entirely."

"Papa, you have not told of the writing of the 'Star-Spangled Banner'!" exclaimed Lulu. "Wasn't it that night it was written?"

"Yes, by Mr. Francis Scott Key, a resident of Georgetown in the District of Columbia, who was at one time a volunteer in the light artillery commanded by Major Peter.

"When the British returned to their vessels after the capture of Washington, they carried with them Dr. Beanes, a well-known physician of Upper Marlborough. Cockburn carried him away onboard the flagship of Admiral Cochrane in spite of the intercession of his friends.

"Then Mr. Key was entreated by the friend to go to Cochrane and intercede for the doctor's release. Key consented, obtained permission of the President, and went under a flag of truce in the cartel ship *Minden* in company with General Skinner.

"When they reached the British fleet it was at the mouth of the Potomac, preparing to attack Baltimore, and though Cochrane agreed to release Dr. Beanes, he refused to let him or his friends return then. They were placed onboard the *Surprise* and courteously treated. The fleet sailed up to the Patapsco, and they were transferred to their own vessel but with a guard of marines to prevent them from landing and communicating with their friends and countrymen.

"Their vessel was anchored in sight of Fort McHenry, and from her deck the American watched the fight, oh, so anxiously! And though it was, as I have said, over before midnight, those anxious watchers did not know until morning how it had ended—whether by surrender of the fort or the abandonment on the part of the enemy of the attempt to take it. It was with anxious hearts they waited for the coming of the dawn, but at last, in the dim light, as the day began to break, their eyes were gladdened by the sight through their glasses directed toward Fort McHenry of the beautiful stars and stripes 'still there,' and to their great joy they soon learned that the attack on Baltimore had failed, that Ross was killed, and the British were returning to their vessels.

"It was while pacing the deck during the great bombardment, full of anxiety for the result that Mr. Key composed the poem that has become so dear to the American heart, 'The Star-Spangled Banner.'"

"Oh, let us sing it!" exclaimed Lulu, and with one consent, patriotic enthusiasm swelling in every heart, they did so, the voices of old and young uniting in the soul-stirring words:

"Oh, say, can you see, by the dawn's early light,
What so proudly we hailed
at the twilight's last gleaming?
Whose broad stripes and bright stars,
through the perilous fight,
O'er the ramparts we watched
were so gallantly streaming

And the rockets' red glare
The bombs bursting in air,
Gave proof through the night
that our flag was still there;
Oh, say, does that star-spangled banner yet wave
O'er the land of the free and the home of the brave?

"On that shore dimly seen
through the mists of the deep,
Where the foe's haughty host in dread silent reposes,
What is that which the breeze,
o'er the towering steep,
As it fitfully blows, now conceals, now discloses?
Now it catches the gleam
Of the morning's first beam,
In full glory reflected, now shines in the stream;

'Tis the star-spangled banner; oh, long may it wave
O'er the land of the free and the home of the brave!

"And where are the foes who so vauntingly swore
That the havoc of war, and the battle's confusion,
A home and a country should leave us no more?
Their blood has washed out
their foul footsteps pollution;
No refuge could save the hireling and slave,
From the terror of flight, or the gloom of the grave;
And the star-spangled banner in triumph doth wave
O'er the land of the free and the home of the brave!

"Oh, thus be it ever, when freemen shall stand
Between their loved homes and the war's desolation!
Blest with vict'ry and peace,
may the heav'n-rescued land
Praise the Pow'r that hath made
and preserved us a nation!
Then conquer we must, when our cause it is just,
And this be our motto, 'In God is our trust!'
And the star-spangled banner in triumph shall wave
O'er the land of the free and the home of the brave!"

A moment of silence followed the dying away of the last strains, then Captain Raymond resumed his narrative, "The first rough words of the song were written by Key upon the back of a letter he happened to have in is pocket, and after his arrival in Baltimore he wrote it out in full. The next morning he read it to his uncle, Judge Nicholson, one of the gallant defenders of the fort, asking his opinion of it. The judge was delighted with it, took it to the printing office of Captain Benjamin Edes, and directed copies be struck off in handbill form. That was done, the handbills were distributed, and it was sung first in the street in front of Edes' office by James Lawrenson, a lad about twelve years of age. That was on the second day after the bombardment of Fort McHenry. The song was 'set up,' printed, and distributed by another lad seventeen or eighteen years old, named Samuel Sands. It created intense enthusiasm, was sung nightly at the theater, and everywhere in public and private."

"Papa," asked Lulu, "what became of the very star-spangled banner Mr. Key was looking for when he wrote the song?"

"I presume it is still in existence," replied her father. "Lossing says it was shown him in Baltimore, during the Civil War, by Christopher Hughes Armistead, the son of the gallant defender of the fort, and that it had in it eleven holes made by the shot of the British during the bombardment."

"Hadn't the British made very sure beforehand of being able to take Baltimore, captain?" asked Evelyn.

"Yes. Their intention was to make it the base for operations. As early as the seventeenth of June a London paper said, 'In the diplomatic circles it is rumored that our naval and military commanders on the American station have no power to conclude any armistice or suspension of arms. They carry with them certain terms which will be offered to the American government at the point of the bayonet. There is reason to believe that America will be left in a much worse situation, as a naval and commercial power, than she was at the commencement of the war.'"

"Ah, how they crowed too soon—before they were out of the woods," laughed Walter. "They needed the lesson they got at Baltimore and the one Jackson gave them some months later at New Orleans."

Chapter Eighth

"Captain, I fear we have been imposing sadly upon your good nature in asking so much history of you in one evening," remarked Grandma Elsie. "You have been extremely kind in complying with the request."

"It has been a pleasure to me, mother," he returned. "There is hardly a subject more interesting to me than the history of my dear native land, and it is my ardent desire to train and teach my children to be earnestly, intelligently patriotic."

"Including your pupils in the list, I presume?" asked Rosie with a saucy smile up into his face.

"Of course, little sister, and as many others as I can influence," was his pleasant rejoinder. "But I am happy to believe that there are few Americans who are not ardent lovers of their own country, considering it the best the sun shines upon."

"As it certainly is, sir!" said Walter. "I'm more thankful than words can express that God gave me my birth in the United States of America."

"As I have no doubt we all are, little brother," said Violet. "But to change the subject. When shall we take that delightful trip to New Orleans? I suppose the sooner the better, that we may not be too much hurried with the necessary dress making?"

"I think so," said her mother, "for both the reason you have given and because the weather will soon become far too unpleasantly warm for shopping in the city."

"You are going with us, mamma?" queried Rosie.

"I really have not thought of it, but probably it would be more prudent for me to stay quietly where I am, Rosie dear," she replied.

"Oh, mamma, we must have you along if you are able to go!" exclaimed Walter. "Please do say that you will."

"Yes, mamma dear, I think it may do you good," said Violet. All the young folks joined urgently in the request that she would make one of the party.

"Perhaps you might, Elsie," her father said in reply to an inquiring look directed at him. "I incline to the opinion that such a change, after your long seclusion here, probably would be of benefit."

"Possibly, father," she said. "Though I had been thinking my staying at home might make Vi more comfortable in leaving her little ones here for a day or two."

"I do not care to go, and I will gladly take charge of the babies if Vi and the captain will trust me with them," Grandma Rose hastened to say. She was warmly thanked by both parents and assured that they would have no hesitation in doing so except on the score of giving her too much care and trouble and missing her pleasant companionship on the contemplated trip.

However, after some further discussion of the matter, it was decided that Mr. and Mrs. Dinsmore would remain at Viamede in charge of house and little ones during the short absence of the others on the contemplated trip.

"Papa, dear papa," Lulu said with tears shining in her eyes and putting her arms lovingly about his neck when he had come into her room to bid her good night, as his custom was, "you are so good to me, your own bad, quick-tempered little daughter! Oh, I do want to be good and make you glad that I belong to you."

"I am that, my daughter, in spite of your faults," he said, caressing her tenderly. "You are very dear to your father's heart, and I am not without hope that you will one day gain full control of the temper that now causes so much pain to both you and me."

"Oh, I do hope I shall, papa, and I want you to punish me every time I indulge it," she said. "But I'm so glad, so thankful to you that you have said I may go with you and the others tomorrow. I feel that I don't deserve it in the least, but I do intend to try as hard as possible to rule my own spirit in the future."

"I am glad to hear it, daughter," the captain responded, imprinting a kiss upon her forehead. "But I must leave you now, for it is growing late and you ought to be in bed that you may be ready to rise in time in the morning."

"Yes, sir. But oh, do stay one minute longer. I—I—" she paused, blushing and a trifle shamefaced.

"What is it, daughter?" he asked, smoothing her hair and cheek caressingly. "Never be afraid to tell your father all that is in your heart."

"Yes, sir. I don't think I'm really afraid—yes, I am a little afraid you might be displeased, and I don't want to do anything to vex or trouble my dear, kind father. But if you're willing, papa, I would like to be allowed to choose for myself what I'm to wear to the wedding."

"Your taste and wishes shall certainly be consulted, daughter," he replied kindly. "Yet I am not prepared to promise that you may have in every case exactly what you would prefer. We must take your mamma and Grandma Elsie into our counsels in order to make sure of getting what will be most becoming and appropriate for you, Lulu."

"Dear me, I would like to be grown up enough to be considered capable of choosing things for myself!" she exclaimed with rueful look and tone. "But, oh, don't be grieved and troubled," as her ear caught the sound of a low-breathed sigh. "I am determined I will be good about it. It certainly would be a very great shame if I were anything else, papa, after all your undeserved goodness to me."

"I do not like to refuse my dear child anything she asks," he said, drawing her into a closer embrace. "But I know too much indulgence would not be for her happiness in the end. And since life is short and uncertain with us all, it may be that she will not be long troubled by being subject to her father's control."

"Oh, papa, please don't talk so!" she exclaimed, sudden tears springing to her eyes. "I can't bear to think of ever losing my own dear, dear father. I hope God may let you live till He is ready to take me, too."

"If He sees best I hope we may long be spared to each other," the captain said, holding her close to his heart. "But now about the matter of which we were speaking. Wise as my dear, eldest daughter considers herself, her father thinks Grandma Elsie and Mamma Vi, by reason of their superior age and knowledge, will be better capable of judging what will be most suitable for her to wear as one of the bridesmaids. And as they are very tasteful in their own dress, and her father is ready to go to any reasonable expense that his dear little girl may be suitably and tastefully attired, and also entirely willing to allow her to decide for herself wherever there is a choice between two or more equally suitable articles, do you not think, as he does, that she should be ready and willing to take what the ladies and he deem most suitable in other things which she would, perhaps, perfer to have somewhat different?"

"Yes, you dear papa," she returned with a look of ardent affection into his eyes. "I do always find out in the end that you know best, and I'd even rather wear any of the dresses I have now than not have you pleased with me, bacause I know I'm never the least bit happy when you are displeased with me."

"Neither am I," he sighed. "It troubles me more than I can tell when my dear daughter Lulu is disobedient and willful. But it is high time you were in bed and resting. God our heavenly Father bless my dear child and keep her safely through the silent watches of the night." Bestowing upon her another tender embrace, he released her and left the room.

She was quite ready for bed, and as she laid her head on her pillow, "Lulu Raymond," she said to herself, "if you do the least thing to vex or trouble that dear father of yours, no punishment he could possibly inflict would be equal to your deserts."

In another minute she was fast asleep, nor did she move again till awakened by some slight sound to find the sun already shining in at her windows.

Her father had directed her the night before what to wear as most suitable for making the trip to the city and back again, and she now made haste in dressing but with the care that he required and that which her own neat taste made desirable. She had just finished when he came in.

"That is right," he said with an approving smile, bending down to give her the usual morning caress. "My little girl looks neat and bright, and I hope is quite well."

"Yes, papa," she returned, putting her arms round his neck and her lips to his in an ardent kiss. "As are you and all the rest, I trust?"

"All, so far as I know, and all who are to take the little trip with us full of pleasurable excitement. We must now go down to breakfast, which is earlier than usual this morning, for we expect the boat in an hour or so."

He took her hand and led her from the room as he spoke. "The others have nearly all gone down already," he added. "There is the bell now. So we have no time to lose."

Lulu, too, was full of pleasurable excitement. "Oh, I'm so glad and thankful to you, papa, that you will let me go!" she exclaimed, lifting to his eyes sparkling with joyous anticipation. "For I know I don't deserve it in the very least. I do intend to be as pleasant-tempered and obedient as possible."

"I don't doubt it, daughter, or expect to have any trouble with you," he said kindly.

By now they had reached the dining room door, morning salutations were exchanged as the different members of the family came flocking in and all quickly took their places at the table, the blessing was asked, and the meal began.

The talk was almost exclusively of what would be seen and done during the trip by those who were to take it, suitable gifts for the bride that was to be, and necessary or desirable shopping for themselves and those remaining at home.

Lulu, sitting beside her father, asked in a low aside, "Papa, may I buy a handsome present for Cousin Betty? I've had occasion to spend hardly any pocket money since we have been here. So I think I've enough to get her something handsome."

"I shall be pleased to have you do so," he replied with a pleasant smile.

"And may I choose it myself?"

"Don't you think it might do well to get some assistance from the rest in making your choice?"

"Oh, yes, sir. Yes, indeed. I really would not want to buy anything you and Grandma Elsie and Mamma Vi thought unsuitable or that would not be likely to please Cousin Betty."

"And may I, too, papa?" asked Gracie, who, seated close to his other side, had overheard a bit of the low-toned talk.

"Yes, indeed, little daughter," he replied, laying a caressing hand upon her head for an instant.

An hour later the little party were all onboard the boat steaming away in the direction of the Gulf, and the talk was more of the beautiful country they were passing through than of the history of that portion yet to be visited. Their route grew more interesting to the young people, and indeed to all, as they came upon scenes made memorable by events in the Revolutionary and Civil Wars and that of 1812–14.

As they passed up the river, the captain pointed out Forts St. Philip and Jackson and other localities connected with the doings and happenings of those times, all gazing upon them as scenes to be indelibly impressed upon the memory of every lover of their dear, native land.

The localities in and about New Orleans connected with the struggle there against the British invaders and aggressors received due attention also and were regarded with equal interest by the young girls and Walter, to say nothing of the older members of the party.

Lulu and Gracie, not to speak of Rosie and Evelyn, who were allowed more latitude in their selection, or of Walter, who was more than willing to trust to "mamma's taste" rather than his own, readily adopted the opinions of papa, Grandma Elsie, and Mamma Vi.

On the evening of their second day in the city, they went to their hotel quite weary enough to enjoy a few hours of rest.

"Mamma, dear," said Violet, glancing at her mother's face as they entered the lower hall. "You do look so fatigued; let us step into this parlor and rest a little before going to our rooms."

"Perhaps it would be as well to do so," replied Mrs. Travilla, following her daughter into the room and sinking wearily into an easy chair that Violet drew forward for her.

"Oh, dear grandma Elsie, how tired you look!" exclaimed Gracie. Walter, speaking at the same instant, said in a tone of deep concern, "Oh, mamma, how pale you are! You must be ill. I wish Cousin Arthur, or some other good doctor, was here to do something to make you feel better."

"Mamma, dear mamma, I fear you are really ill!" exclaimed Rosie in a tone of anxiety, while Lulu ran back into the hall in search of her father, who had stepped aside to the clerk's desk to attend to some business matter—for to her he was a tower of strength to be flown to in every need.

But an elderly lady and gentleman, the only other occupants of the parlor at the moment, hastily rose and drew near the little group, the lady saying in a tone of mingled concern and delight, "It is my Cousin Elsie—Mrs. Travilla—I am sure! You know me, dear cousin? Mildred Keith—Mrs. Landreth? And this is my husband, the doctor. I think he could do something to relieve you."

"Cousin Mildred! Oh, what a joyful surprise! How glad I am to see you!" exclaimed Mrs. Travilla, the color coming back to her cheek and the light back to her eyes, as she raised herself to a sitting posture and threw her arms about Mildred's neck.

The two held each other in a long, tender embrace, hardly conscious for the moment of the presence of the others, who stood looking on in surprise and delight, Captain Raymond and Lulu having joined the group.

Then mutual introductions and joyous greetings followed, questions about absent dear ones were asked and answered, and each party learned that the other was in the city for but a brief sojourn, purposing to go thence to Viamede or its near vicinity.

In the meanwhile Mrs. Travilla seemed to have forgotten her weariness and exhaustion, and she was looking more than ordinarily young and bright.

Dr. Landreth remarked it with a pleased smile. "I am glad to meet you, Cousin Elsie," he said. "Though you seem no longer in need of my services as physician."

"No, indeed, Cousin Charlie," she returned brightly. "You are so excellent a doctor that your presence, especially when accompanied by that of your wife," with a smiling glance at Mildred, "does one good like a medicine."

"Still, if you will allow it, I will prescribe," he said, "an hour's rest on a couch in your own room to be followed by a substantial meal either there or at the table with the rest of us."

"Exactly the prescription I should give were I your physician, mother," said Captain Raymond. "May I not assist you to your room?"

"Yes," she said with a smile. "As I know Dr. Landreth to be an excellent physician I shall follow his advice, confidently expecting to profit by so doing. Doctor," turning to him, "we have a pleasant private parlor where we take our meals and enjoy each other's society in the intervals of sightseeing and shopping. I hope you and Cousin Mildred will join us at mealtimes, and at all times when you find it agreeable, making yourselves perfectly at home. Now, goodbye for the present. I hope to be able, after an hour's rest, to join you all at the tea table."

With evident pleasure her invitation was accepted. An hour later she made her appearance in the parlor, much refreshed by rest and sleep; a tempting meal was partaken of by all with evident appetite; the remainder of the evening passed in delightful social exchange; and all retired early that they might be ready for a long day of interesting and, to the children especially, captivating shopping. As Rosie remarked, "Nothing could be more enjoyable than the business of selecting wedding gifts and pretty things to be worn at the wedding festivities."

She was quite delighted with her own finery and presents for Betty, selected by herself with her mother's assistance, Violet occasionally giving her opinion or advice, Mrs. Landreth and the gentlemen doing the same when asked. They consisted of handsome jewelry and silver.

Walter, too, chose, with his mother's help, a set of gold-lined silver spoons for his cousin Betty. Evelyn's gift was a handsome silver pie knife and salt spoons. Lulu, too, and Gracie gave silver and also a pair of beautiful gold bracelets. The captain's own gift was an expensive set of jewelry; Violet's a lovely bridal veil; Grandma Elsie's a beautiful and costly diamond pin, to which she afterward added a check for five thousand dollars. Also Dr. and Mrs. Landreth bought as their gift some very handsome articles of dress and house furnishings.

The shopping and a little sight seeing filled up the time till Saturday, when they returned to Viamede by the same boat that had brought the captain and his party to the city.

It was a very warm and joyous welcome that awaited them there from Grandpa and Grandma Dinsmore and little Elsie and Ned Raymond, and none the less joyous was the greeting given Dr. and Mrs. Landreth by their relatives and old friends, Mr. and Mrs. Dinsmore.

To each of the four it was a delightful reunion, and much of the evening was passed in recalling the events of their exchanges in those early days when Elsie and her cousin Annis were happy children together, these older ones merry, young married folks, and the eldest son of each couple but a baby boy, though now each was the head of a young family of his own.

These reminiscences were very interesting to themselves, Grandma Elsie, and the Keiths, who had been invited to Viamede to take tea with these relatives and who were to go to the parsonage for a short stay with the others.

But after a little the young folks grew tired of listening to the talk and sought out another part of the veranda where they could converse among themselves without disturbing their elders.

Captain Raymond's eyes followed the movements of his little girls with a look of fond fatherly pride, not without a shade of anxiety as they noted the weariness in Gracie's face. Presently he rose and drew near the little group.

"Gracie, my darling, do you not want to go to your bed?" he asked. "I think my little girl is looking tired and would be better for a long night's rest."

"Yes, papa, I am 'most too tired to keep my eyes open," she replied with a faint smile up at his face.

"Then come, my dear," he said, bending down and taking her in his arms. "I will carry you to your room and bid the others good night for you when I come down again. You are too tired to wait to do that yourself," and he carried her away.

Lulu sprang up and ran after them. "Shall I go, too, papa?" she asked.

"If you, too, feel too tired to stay up for prayers," he answered pleasantly. "Otherwise I would not have you absent from that service."

"Yes, sir. I'm not too tired. Good night, Gracie," she said and ran back to her mates.

Their tongues were running on the old theme of the wedding so soon to take place, gifts to the bride, and dresses to be worn by her and her attendants. But all of them were pretty well worn out with the shopping and traveling gone through in the last few days, seeing which their elders thought it best to hold the evening service a little earlier than usual, then retire to rest.

"Papa, please may I ask a few questions now, before you leave me?" Lulu entreated when he came in to bid her good night.

"Yes," he replied with an amused look. "That is number one. How many are to follow?" seating himself and drawing her to his knee.

"Oh, I don't know exactly, sir. It will depend somewhat upon the answers, I think," she returned laughingly, putting an arm round his neck and kissing him with her usual display of affection.

"Then let me go through the ordeal as soon as possible," he responded, patting her cheek and pressing his lips to hers.

"I hope it won't be a very dreadful ordeal to you, papa," she said, smiling up into his eyes. "First, then, are we to have school as usual between this and the time of the wedding?"

"Yes," was the prompt, decided reply.

"Oh, dear!" she said between a sigh and a laugh, "I 'most wish you were one of the fathers that could be coaxed. But, oh, please don't begin to look sorry and grave. I'm determined I will be good about that and everything—just as good as I know how to be—and if I'm not I just hope you'll punish me well, only not by refusing to allow me to act as bridesmaid to Cousin Betty."

"Love to your father and a desire to please him seems to me a far better motive for good behavior than fear of punishment," he said with a grave look and tone.

"Yes, sir. That is my motive. Please believe it, my own dear father," she said, lifting dewy eyes to his.

"Then I have strong hope that my pleasure in the coming festivities will not be spoiled by having a naughty, rebellious little daughter to deal with or an idle one, either. Now what else?"

"Only this, papa. That if you should have letters to write you will let me help you, using my own typewriter, you know."

"Thank you, my dear little helpful daughter. Should I find that I have letters you could answer for me in that way, I will call upon you for your offered assistance, as I well know it will be a pleasure to you to render it," he replied with a smile and another tender caress. "I hope you feel no doubt that it is not for lack of love for his dear child your father refuses the holiday you have asked for."

"No indeed, papa. I know you love me dearly. It would break my heart to think you didn't."

"As it would mine to think my little girl did not love me. Now you must go at once to bed. Good night and pleasant dreams."

Chapter Ninth

*I*t was early morning at Ion, breakfast awaiting the return of Mr. Edward Travilla, who had ridden into the village on some business errand, leaving word that he would be back within the hour to partake of the morning meal with his wife.

Zoe, tastefully attired, was on the veranda, and the twin babies, fresh from their bath, looking, the young mother averred, like little angels in their dainty white robes, were toddling about there— laughing, cooing, and prattling. They were the idols of her heart. She romped and played with them now, but with frequent pauses to listen for the sound of the horse's hoofs or gaze down the avenue, saying in joyous tones to the babies, "Papa is coming, coming soon—your dear, dear papa! And mamma and his darlings will be so glad to see him. Ah, there he is at last!" she added at length, as a horseman turned in at the great gates and came at a quick canter up the avenue.

He lifted his hat with a bow and smile to his wife as he drew near. Then alighting at the steps, where a servant took the reins and led the horse away, he hastily ascended them, and the next moment he was seated with a little one upon each knee.

"Papa's darlings!" he said, caressing them in turn. "Papa's dear darlings!"

"Tell papa we have been wanting him," said Zoe, standing alongside, smoothing Edward's hair with softly caressing hand, and smiling down fondly into the faces of the three. "Tell him he stayed so long we did not know how to wait."

"I must acknowledge I am a trifle late, my dear," Edward said, smiling up into the pretty rosy face. "I was detained by business, but here is my atonement," handing her a telegram, which he took from his pocket.

Zoe read it aloud. It was an invitation to a wedding—whose it did not say—at Viamede to take place in three weeks from that day.

"Why, who on earth can be going to be married?" she exclaimed in surprise. "Rosie? Evelyn? Lulu? Everyone of them is too young." Then with a look into Edward's laughing eyes, "Now you needn't laugh, Ned. I know and acknowledge that Rosie is a little older than I was when we married, but we would not have made such haste except under those peculiar circumstances."

"Quite true, my dear," he responded. "I suppose you will hardly think it necessary to decline the invitation on that account?"

"Oh, no indeed," came the laughing rejoinder. "I am altogether in favor of accepting and shall begin my preparations at once. But there's the breakfast bell, my darling."

When they had fairly begun their meal, the subject was renewed and Edward remarked, "My dear, you will want a new dress. If you'd like, we will drive into the city this morning, make all of the necessary purchases, and at once set Alma or some other dressmaker at work."

"Oh, thank you, Ned," she returned, her eyes shining with pleasure. "No woman ever had a more generous husband than mine. But there are so many ways for your money to go, and I have several that would be—with remodeling and retrimming—as tasteful, handsome, and becoming as any new one."

"But you must have a new one, my love," Edward replied decidedly. "I can easily afford it, and it is a great pleasure to me to see my little wife well and becomingly dressed."

"A very nice speech, my dear husband," returned Zoe laughingly. "Really I have not the heart to refuse you the pleasure of seeing your wife arrayed in finery just suited to your taste. So I am very glad you are willing to go with me and assist in the selection. Shall we take the babies along?"

"To help with the shopping? I doubt if we would find them of any assistance."

"They are good little things though and would not be any hindrance," returned the young mother laughingly. "But the trip might interfere with their morning nap, so if you think best, we will leave the darlings at home."

"I really think they would have a more comfortable time," Edward said. "We also. Hark! There's the telephone. Excuse me a moment, my dear."

"Certainly, my love, but as I may possibly be the one wanted, I'll go along by your leave," she added laughingly, running after him as he left the room.

The call proved to be from Mrs. Elsie Leland. A telegram from Viamede had reached them also, and they would be at Ion in the course of an hour to talk over necessary arrangements for the journey, if, as they supposed, Edward and Zoe would like to take it in company with them. They, too, were invited, of course?

"Yes," Edward answered. "Our mamma would certainly not neglect her eldest son at such a time. Come over as soon as you like, as we are prepared to drive into the city to make necessary purchases before setting the dressmakers at work upon suitable adornments for the ladies of our party."

"Nothing at all to be bought for the gentlemen, I suppose?" was Elsie's response, accompanied by a low, sweet laugh. "We will be happy to accept your invitation. Goodbye till then."

"Now, let us go back and finish our breakfast," said Zoe. "If the Lelands are to be here in an hour we have no time to spare."

They were turning away when the bell rang again.

It was Ella Conly who called this time. The same invitation for herself and brothers had just been received. They knew that Ned and Zoe must of course have shared the summons to Viamede, and, if convenient, they would call at Ion after tea that evening to talk over plans and preparations.

They were cordially urged to do so. Then Edward called to his Uncle Horace at the Oaks, his Aunt Rose at the Laurels, and Aunt Lora Howard at Pinegrove and learned to his satisfaction that all had received and would accept the same invitation. But they had not yet settled upon their plans in regard to the needed preparations and the time of setting out upon the journey.

Edward suggested that it might be satisfactory for all to meet at Ion that evening and talk the matter over—an invitation which was promptly accepted by all.

"Now let us finish our breakfast," Edward said, leading the way back to the table.

"Yes," said Zoe. "I am sure that I for one have no time to waste if I'm to be ready to start for the city in an hour."

She was ready, however, when, in less than an hour, the Fairview carriage drove up bringing the Lelands. Elsie declined an invitation to alight. "We have none too much time now," she said, "for shopping cannot always be done in haste, and we are not making a very early start. Just get in here with us, you two, will you not? There's plenty of room, and we can talk over matters and settle plans as we drive."

"A very good idea, and we are much obliged," returned Edward, handing Zoe in and taking a seat by her side.

"Who is to be married, Elsie?" asked Zoe. "Surely it could not be mamma herself?" she added with a light laugh. "I feel quite sure she would not accept the best and greatest man upon earth."

"And I feel as sure of that as you do," said Mrs. Leland. "She thinks of my father not as lost to her but waiting for her to rejoin him in the better land. I have been trying to think who the coming bride is to be and suppose it is Betty Johnson."

"But it may be that the groom and not the bride belongs to our family," remarked Lester. "Who would be more likely than Dick Percival?"

"Why, yes, to be sure!" exclaimed Edward. "It is about time Dick had a wife. Mother would of course be interested and ready to do anything in her power to make it pleasant for him and his new wife."

"I should really like to know more about it before choosing gifts for her," remarked Zoe.

"I, too," said Elsie.

"Then suppose we let that wait for another day and content ourselves with purchasing what is needed for the adorning of you two ladies," suggested Edward. And that was what, after a little further consultation, was decided upon.

The city was reached in safety, and some hours later they returned, as Zoe said, "Laden with lovely things for their own adornment."

The babies were on the veranda waiting and watching eagerly for papa and mamma, who, their nurse kept telling them, would soon be seen coming down the avenue. When they did appear, alighting from the Fairview carriage, they were recognized with a glad cry, and Zoe, forgetting her weariness, ran to the little ones, embraced first one and then the other, put a toy in the hand of each, spent another minute or two caressing them, then hurried to her own apartments to dress for tea and the family gathering expected in the evening.

Elsie and her husband had driven home, but they would return for the informal assembly of the members of the connection.

The guests came early, Ella Conley and her brothers from Roselands being the first. Ella was in high glee. She had long felt an ardent desire to visit Viamede, and now she hailed with delight the opportunity to do so. The circumstances of both brothers had greatly improved, and they were disposed to be very generous to the only sister remaining at home with them, and they had told her she must have a new, handsome dress for the wedding and everything else she needed to fit her out well for the journey and a sojourn of some weeks at Viamede.

Zoe felt flattered by being consulted in regard to necessary or desirable purchases and greatly enjoyed exhibiting her own and describing Elsie's of that day.

Then the other families, or delegates from them, arrived in rapid succession, and a merry sociable interview ensued. All were quite resolved, should nothing interfere, to accept the invitation to Viamede, but some of them could not yet decide upon the exact time when they would be prepared to leave their homes for that distant point and for an absence of several weeks. But the Ion, Oaks, Fairview, and Roselands people would all go in two weeks in company. It was still early when wheels were heard approaching from the direction of the village. A hack turned in at the gate, drove rapidly up the avenue, halted at the veranda steps, and an old gentleman alighted.

"Cousin Ronald!" exclaimed Elsie Leland, Edward, and Zoe in a breath, and they and the others gathered about him with words of both cordial greeting and gracious welcome.

"You have given us a most pleasant surprise, Cousin Ronald," Edward said when the old gentleman was comfortably seated in an easy chair. "You have not been to tea?"

"Yes, laddie, I took that in the village where I alighted frae the cars. But the auld folks seem to be missing here," glancing about in search of them as he spoke. "I dinna see your honored grandsire, his wife, or my sweet Cousin Elsie, your mither. The bairns Rosie and Walter, too, are not here. What's become o' them a', laddie? They're no ill, I hope?"

"They were quite well at last accounts, sir," replied Edward. "They have spent the winter and early spring at Viamede, and they will not return for some weeks yet."

"Ah ha! Um h'm! Ah ha!" murmured the older gentleman reflectively. "It's no the best o' news to me—an auld mon who has been wearyin' for a sight o' your mother's sweet face."

"Don't say that, cousin, for we are going there ourselves, and we shall be glad indeed to take you with us. I know of no one who would be a more welcome guest to my mother."

"Have a care, sir, that ye dinna tempt an auld mon too far," laughed Cousin Ronald.

"Oh, but you must go with us, sir," said Zoe. "What would mamma say if we failed to bring you? Besides, we want your company even if mamma would not be displeased were you not with us."

"Ah ha! Um h'm! Ah ha! Weel, my bony leddy, I canna refuse an invitation that holds out so great a prospect of enjoyment."

"No, you mustn't think of refusing, Cousin Ronald!" exclaimed Edward and Elsie together.

"Indeed no," said Mr. Horace Dinsmore. "We can assure you of a hearty welcome, and my sister, as Zoe says, would be by no means pleased should we fail to take you along with us. But since the first division of our company does not start for two weeks, there will be abundance of time to hear from her on the subject."

"Certainly there will, uncle," responded Edward. "I shall write to mamma tonight. Several of us have heard from her today by telegraph, Cousin Ronald, and we think we shall surely have letters soon."

Then followed the story of the telegrams received that day, and the guesses and surmises as to whose wedding they were invited to attend.

Mr. Lilburn was evidently much interested and more than willing to yield to their persuasions to accompany them to Viamede.

"Well, friends and cousins," he said, "there is scarce anything I can think of at this moment that would delight me more than to gang with you to see them at that lovely spot—an earthly paradise, as it may well be called. I am somewhat fatigued now, but rest for a few days—the days that must come and go afore we start—will no doubt supply the needed strength for the new journey. And the wedding festivities to follow will not come amiss even to a man of my ain venerable age."

"No, indeed!" exclaimed Zoe. "I should think not. Surely people of any age may enjoy merry, festive scenes and doings. It has always been a source of regret to me that Edward's and my nuptials were graced by none of them."

"Possibly there may be better luck for you next time," remarked Edward laughingly.

"Indeed I want no next time," she returned with spirit. "I've no intention of trying a second husband lest I might do worse than I did in taking you."

"It strikes me there might be a possibility of doing very much worse, my dear niece," remarked Mr. Horace Dinsmore pleasantly.

"As it does me," responded Zoe, with a proudly affectionate look into her young husband's eyes.

"I am glad to hear it," was his remark, given with an affectionate glance into the bright, sweet face.

For the next two weeks Zoe and the other ladies of the connection were very delightfully busy with their preparations for the journey wedding.

Letters had come telling that Betty was, as had been conjectured, the prospective bride, who was to be the groom, where the ceremony was to take place, the bridal feast to be partaken of and other interesting particulars. The dresses of bride, bridesmaids, and maids of honor were not described, as they would be seen by all the relatives at, if not before, the wedding.

The journey to New Orleans was made by rail. From thence they took a steamboat for Berwick Bay, preferring to make the rest of the journey by water. The party consisted of the Dinsmores, Lelands, Travillas, Conleys, and their Aunt Adelaide, Mrs. Allison of Philadelphia, who had come on from her home shortly before to join these relatives in their trip to Louisiana. She, too, had been urgently invited to attend the wedding. And last but not least was Mr. Ronald Lilburn.

They were a very cheerful set—the younger ones quite merry and mirthful. There were only a few other passengers, among whom was a lady clad in deep mourning—widow's weeds—who kept her face carefully concealed by her thick crepe veil and sat apart. She seemed to studiously avoid all contact with her fellow passengers, observing which, the other passengers respectfully refrained from making advances toward acquaintanceship. But now and then Dr. Conley turned an observing eye upon her. There was a droop about her figure that struck him as an indication of illness or exhaustion from some other cause.

At length he rose, and stepping to her side, said in a low, sympathizing tone, "I fear you are ill, madam. I am a physician, and if I can do anything for you my services are at your command."

She made an inarticulate reply in tones quivering with emotion, staggered to her feet as she spoke, made one step forward, and would have fallen had he not caught her with his arm.

Her head dropped upon his shoulder, and instantly the other members of his party gathered about them with excited exclamations. "What is the matter?" "Is she ill?" "Do you know her, Art? She has fainted, has she not?" The last exclamation and query came from the lips of Mrs. Elsie Leland.

"Yes. She is quite unconscious," came Arthur's low-toned reply. "And this thick, heavy veil is smothering her."

The next instant he had at last succeeded in disentangling it. With a quick movement he threw it back, lifted the seemingly lifeless form, laid it on a settee with the head low, laid his finger on her pulse for an instant, then began compressing the ribs and allowing them to expand again.

"I will have to loosen her clothing," he said, leaning over her to do so. Then for the first time catching sight of her face, he started back with a low, pained exclamation, "My sister Virginia! Is it possible?"

"Virginia!" exclaimed Adelaide and Calhoun in a breath, for both were standing near. "Can it be?" The others exchanged glances of astonishment, then Ella asked in low, terrified tones, "Oh, Art, is she—is she dead? Poor, poor Virgie!"

"No. It is only a faint," he answered, going on with his efforts to restore consciousness, in which he was presently successful.

Virginia's eyes opened, looked up into his with evident recognition of her brother, then closed, while tears stole down her cheeks. He leaned over her in brotherly solicitude.

"Virgie, my poor, dear sister," he said in tones tremulous with emotion, "you are with relatives and friends who will gladly do anything and everything in their power for your comfort and happiness. I think you are not well—"

She seemed to be making an effort to speak, and, leaving his sentence unfinished, he bent down over her with his ear almost touching her lips.

"Starving," was the whispered word that came in reply, and he started back aghast, his features working with emotion.

"Can it be possible!" was his half-suppressed exclamation from his lips.

"What is it?" asked Calhoun. "What does she say?"

"She is faint and ill with hunger," returned his brother in a moved tone. "Get me a glass of hot milk as quickly as you can, Cal." And Calhoun hurried away in quest of it.

In a few minutes he was back again with a large tumbler of rich, sweet milk, which Virginia drank with avidity. Some more substantial food was then given her, and after a little she was able to exchange greetings with the other relatives onboard and to give some account of herself.

"Henry Neuville is dead, and I set out on my journey to beg a home with Isa as soon as I had seen him laid decently away," she said. "I have no means at all—unfortunate creature that I am—but perhaps I can make myself useful enough to earn my bread."

"Your brothers will be both able and willing to clothe you," said the doctor and Calhoun added, "Certainly, and to give you a home, too, should Isa and her husband find it inconvenient to do so."

At that tears coursed down Virginia's cheeks.

"You are good, kind brothers," she said. "You are far better to me than I deserve. But living with a man of the stamp of Henry Neuville has taught me how to appreciate true gentlemen."

"Oh, Virgie, did he die as he had lived?" asked her cousin, Elsie.

"I saw no sign of repentance or reformation," returned Virginia. "He died of drink with curses on his tongue. I can't mourn his loss. How could I? But I'm the most unfortunate woman—the poorest in the whole connection. I wasn't brought up to support myself either, and I can't do it."

"Perhaps you may yet learn how," said Zoe encouragingly. "There are a great many avenues of self-support now open to women, you know."

A look of disgust and annoyance was Virginia's only response to that.

A few moments of silence ensued, broken only by the prattle of the little ones, and then there was a sudden sound as of some heavy body plunging into the water accompanied by the shrill cry, "Man overboard!"

A great commotion instantly followed, the captain giving his orders to lower a boat and go in search of the man and at the same time slowing the movements of the steamer.

The party were much interested and excited, most of them full of concern for the drowning one, who seemed to have strangely disappeared, for not a trace of him could be seen as the boat rowed hither and thither. At length, resigning all hope of finding even the lifeless body, the men returned to the larger vessel to report their failure.

The ladies were in tears, and as the captain drew near, Zoe asked in tones tremulous with emotion, "Oh, is there no hope at all of saving the poor fellow, captain?"

"I'm afraid he's gone to the bottom, ma'am, though it's odd he couldn't keep up for the few minutes it took to launch the boat. But I suppose the wheel must have struck him. By the way," he added, as if struck by a sudden thought, "I don't know yet who it was. I must have the crew mustered on deck and see who is missing."

He proceeded to do so, when, to the surprise of all it was discovered that no one was missing.

"A stowaway, evidently!" growled the captain. "And he's got his deserts, though I wouldn't have let him drown if I could have helped it."

At that instant a light broke upon Edward Travilla and Dr. Conley, and both turned hastily toward their guest, Mr. Ronald Lilburn.

He was sitting near, listening to the talk, his features expressing grave concern, yet they could perceive a sparkle of fun in his eye.

Edward stepped to his side, and, bending down over him, spoke in an undertone close to his ear. "I think you could tell us something of the man, Cousin Ronald."

"I, laddie? What would I ken o' the folk in this part o' the world?" queried the old gentleman, raising his eyebrows in mock surprise.

"Ah, sir, who is to say he belonged to this part of the world?" laughed Edward. "I must own that I strongly suspect he was a countryman of yours—a Scotsman, at least."

Then going to the side of his wife he said a word or two in an undertone that chased away her tears, while she immediately sent a laughing glance in Cousin Ronald's direction.

They were drawing near their journey's end, and presently everything else seemed to be forgotten in gazing upon the ever-changing beauties of the landscape as they threaded their way through lake and lakelet, past swamp, forest, plain, and plantation. They gazed with delight upon the cool, shady dells carpeted with a rich growth of flowers, miles upon miles of smoothly shaven lawns—velvety green and shaded by magnificent oaks and magnolias, lordly villas peering through groves of orange trees, tall white sugarhouses, and the long rows of cabins of the laborers, forming all together a panorama of surpassing loveliness.

"It is an earthly paradise, is it not, Ned?" cried Zoe, clasping her hands in an ecstasy of delight.

"Very, very beautiful," he responded, his eyes shining with pleasure. "But you know this is not, like yours, my first sight of it. I spent a very happy winter here in the days when my dear and honored father was with us."

"And I," said his sister Elsie, softly sighing at the thought that that loved parent had left them to return no more. "It will not seem the same without him. Yet with so many dear ones—especially our dear, dear mother—our visit can hardly be otherwise than most enjoyable. Ah, Ned, is not that our own orange orchard just coming into view?"

"It is, my dear sister. We will be there in a few minutes now."

"At home and with mamma!" she exclaimed in joyous tones, then called to her sons, "Come here, Ned and Eric. We are almost to dear grandmamma's house, and she will soon have you in her arms."

At that the little fellows came running to her with a joyous shout, for they dearly loved their Grandma Elsie, and to their infant minds the time of separation from her had seemed very long.

To their Aunt Adelaide, the Conleys—Arthur excepted—and the young Dinsmores the scenes were equally new and called forth from one and all demonstrations of admiration and delight. Very soon the boat reached and rounded to at the landing, where were gathered all the members of the Viamede, Magnolia Hall, and parsonage families to meet and welcome these dear ones from their own old homes farther to the north.

It was an altogether joyous meeting, Cousin Ronald and Virginia, as well as the rest, receiving a most kind and cordial greeting, though the latter was an entirely unexpected guest.

Isadore took her sister in her arms, kissed, and wept over her as a near and dear one who had gone through great trials during the years of their separation.

"What a long, long while it is since we parted, and what sore trials you have gone through in the meantime, Virgie!" she sighed. "Ah, I hope the future may have better things in store for you."

"I should say it ought, indeed, considering all I've had to suffer in the past," returned Virginia. "I've come to beg a home with you, Isa. I suppose as you might have had to do of me if I had been the lucky one in the matter of drawing a prize in the matrimonial lottery."

"I will try to do the very best I can for you, Virgie," was Isadore's pleasant-toned reply, though it was not with unmingled satisfaction that she saw opening before her the prospect of receiving this selfish, indolent sister into her peaceful and well regulated household as a permanent addition to it.

Zoe was in ecstasies over the beauties of Viamede—the large, palatial mansion, the beautiful grounds, the lovely scenery.

"Oh, mamma," she exclaimed, pausing on the veranda to take a general survey, "it is just too lovely for anything! It really exceeds my expectations, though they were raised very high by all I have heard of the beauties of Viamede. I wonder you can ever resign yourself to leaving it for a longer time than the hot season, when it is not so healthy as your more northern home."

"Yes, I sometimes wonder at myself," Elsie said with a smile. "And yet both Ion and the Oaks are very dear to me—so many happy years of my life have been passed in them. Ah, no, I could not give up those dear homes entirely any more than I could this."

"Ah, you are a most fortunate woman, cousin mine," remarked Mr. Lilburn, standing by. "And worthy of it all; no one more so."

"Ah, Cousin Ronald, you, like all the rest of my friends, are only too ready to pass my imperfections by and see only virtues—some of them altogether imaginary, I fear," she returned with a smile. "I cannot tell you how glad I am to see you here again, and I hope you may so greatly enjoy your sojourn among us that you will be pleased to repeat your visit whenever opportunity offers."

"Many thanks, cousin, but I have a care lest you should be in danger of seeing me here oftener than will be found agreeable," came his laughing reply.

At that Elsie shook her head with a playful smile, then turned to baby Lily, who was reaching out her little arms to grandma, crying, "Take, take, gamma!"

"No, no, mother dear," Edward said, coming up to them and taking his little daughter from the nurse's arms. "I can't have you wearying yourself with her." Then to the child, "Papa is going to carry you upstairs, little darling. Dear grandma has been sick and is not strong enough to carry you about. The friends and relatives will all be here for some time, mother?" turning to her again.

"Yes," she replied. "They will all stay to tea."

"Zoe and I will join you and them again in a few minutes," he said, moving on through the hall in the direction of the stairway.

All scattered to their rooms then, but they reassembled on the veranda for some few minutes before the call to the tea table. It was a large, merry, informal tea party, Grandma Elsie having been most hospitably urgent that everyone should stay, partake with her and the others who had been making Viamede their home for months past, and spend the evening.

The approaching wedding and matters connected with it were naturally the principal themes of discourse, and Betty was good-humoredly rallied on the conquest she had made and the pleasant prospect of having a home of her own with at least one loyal subject. Zoe insisted on a description of the trousseau, especially the wedding dress.

"Drive over to Magnolia Hall day after tomorrow and you shall see everything for yourself, Zoe," Betty said, laughing and blushing. "At least all but the gifts that have not yet come in."

"Thank you. I think I'll accept that invitation," returned Zoe. "But I suppose there is something to be seen here?"

"Yes, the dresses of the bridesmaids and maids of honor," said Rosie. "And we who are to wear them think them quite beautiful. Don't we, girls?" turning toward Evelyn and Lulu, who answered with an emphatic, "Yes, indeed!"

"Suppose you come and take a look at them, Zoe," proposed Rosie, as they left the table, and Zoe promptly accepted the invitation. Betty, Elsie Leland, Ella, Virginia, and the Dinsmore cousins all went along as well.

"Oh, they are lovely!" was the united exclamation at sight of the dresses. Zoe added, "I can't say which is handsomest."

"That's just how it is with me," laughed Betty. "But I own to thinking the bride's dress a trifle handsomer than any of these."

"Yes, but just think how we may outshine you when our turns come to wear a wedding dress," said Rosie. "I mean to have one that shall be a marvel of beauty and taste. Don't you, Eva and Lu?"

"I very much doubt whether I shall ever have any," replied Evelyn with her grave, sweet smile.

"If you don't it will be your own fault, I am sure," said Rosie. "And it will be just the same with Lu."

"I'm not going to get married ever!" cried Lulu emphatically. "I wouldn't leave my father for all the rest of the men in all the world."

"Ah, your father is glad to hear it," said a voice close at her side, while a hand was laid affectionately on her shoulder. "But my own dear, eldest daughter is still quite too young to be even thinking of such things."

"Then I won't think of them if I can help it, papa dear," she said, lifting loving, smiling eyes to his face, "for indeed I do want to obey even your slightest wish."

"I don't doubt it, daughter," he returned, pressing affectionately the hand she had slipped into his.

"Now, Elsie," said Zoe, addressing Mrs. Leland, "let us show our wedding finery. You, Ella Conley, I suppose won't care to open your trunks, as they are to be carried over to the parsonage."

"They have already gone," said Isadore, she also having joined the party of inspection. "But all of the finery can be shown there just as well."

"Yes, it can wait," returned Ella. "And perhaps it will be all the more appreciated for not being seen along with so many other beauties."

"I am the only one who has no finery to exhibit," remarked Virginia in an ill-used tone. But they were already on their way to Mrs. Leland's room, and no one seemed to hear or heed the complaint, everybody being too much engrossed with the business in hand to take notice of her ill-humor.

It was Saturday evening, and the parsonage and Magnolia Hall people returned to their homes at an early hour, taking their guests with them.

"Now, daughter," Captain Raymond said, turning at once to Lulu as the last carriage disappeared from sight, "go at once to your own room and prepare for bed."

"Yes, sir. Must I say good night now to you?" she asked in a low tone, close at his ear.

"No," he returned with a smile. "I will be with you presently for a few minutes."

She looked her thanks and hastened to obey.

"I am quite ready for bed, papa," she said when he came into her room. "Please mayn't I sit on your knee for five or ten minutes?"

"That is just what I want to do," he said, taking possession of an easy chair and drawing her to the coveted place. "I must have a little talk with my dear, eldest daughter," he continued, smoothing her hair and cheek caressingly.

"What about, papa, dear?" she asked, nestling closer in his arms. "I haven't been misbehaving, have I? You are not displeased with me, are you?"

"No, dear child. I am only afraid that you may be caring too much about dress and finery, and that perhaps I am not altogether blameless in regard to that. I may not have guarded my dear little girls against it as I should."

"I am afraid that perhaps I do care too much about it, papa dear," she sighed, hanging her head, while blushes dyed her cheek. "But I'm sure it is all my own fault, not yours at all. So, please don't feel badly about it."

He took up her Bible, opened it, and read, "'Whose adorning, let it not be that outward adorning of plaiting the hair, and of wearing of gold, or of putting on apparel; but let it be the hidden man of the heart, in that which is not corruptible, even the ornament of a meek and quiet spirit, which is in the sight of God of great price. For after this manner in the old time the holy women also, who trusted in God, adorned themselves.'"

"Papa, is it wrong to wear nice, pretty clothes, and to enjoy having them?" she asked, as he closed the book and laid it aside. "Is that what is meant in those verses?"

"I think not," he said. "If I understood it in that way I should feel wrong to allow a daughter of mine to wear them. I think it means that you are not to care too much about such adornment, but more, much more, for that other and greater adornment, even the hidden man of the heart, the ornament of a meek and quiet spirit, remembering that in the sight of God it is of great price, worth infinitely more than any ornament of gold, the richest jewels, or the finest attire. Cultivate that with all diligence, my own darling child, if you desire to please and honor your heavenly Father and make yourself even dearer than you now are to your earthly one, and lovelier in his eyes."

"Oh, I do, papa! I do want to please and honor God, and you too; I want to be just a joy and blessing and comfort to you, my own dear, dear father! I don't think you have any idea how very, very dearly I love you, papa," putting her arms about his neck and kissing him over and over again. "Gracie and I think indeed we feel quite sure that no other children ever had such a dear, good, kind father as ours. And I know Max thinks the same."

"Well, daughter, I delight in having you and all my children think so, however mistaken you maybe," he said, with a pleased smile, holding her close and returning her caresses; "and it certainly is the earnest desire of my heart to be the best, kindest, and dearest of fathers to the darling children God has given me."

"As I am sure you are, dear papa," she said. "I never have any doubt of it at all, even when you punish me. And, papa," she added, with an effort, "if you think finery bad for me, I am willing to be dressed just as plainly as you think best."

"That is my own dear little girl," he returned, with a gratified look; "but I have not been dressing you better more richly, gayly, or tastefully than seems to me right and proper; also, I think quite as much sin may be committed by being proud of plainness in dress as proud of wearing finery. What I am aiming at is to have my little daughter look upon dress as a secondary matter, and feel far more anxious to be one who is pleasing in the sight of her heavenly

Father than one admired and envied by some earthly creature as the possessor of wealth, and fine or costly raiment. In short, I want you to feel that the style and richness of your attire is a matter of little consequence, while to live in the light of God's countenance, pleasing and honoring Him and growing in holiness and conformity to His will, is to be desired and striven for beyond everything else."

"Yes, papa," she said softly, "I will ask God to help me to do so; and you will pray for me too, won't you?"

"Indeed I will, my darling; we will kneel down and ask him now; ask for help to keep from indulging in worldly mindedness and vanity, and that our earnest desire and effort may ever be to serve and honor and glorify him in all our words and ways."

"My own dear father," she said, when they had risen from their knees, "I am sure that if I don't grow up a good Christian the fault will not be yours." Then, glancing at the bed where Grace lay in a profound sleep, "I am so glad and thankful that I am not feeble like poor, dear Gracie, because if I had to go to bed and to sleep so early as she almost always does, I'd miss these nice talks from you. But, fortunately, she doesn't need so much help to be good as I do, Ah, papa, I've given you a great deal more trouble to train me up right than she ever has, or will."

"My darling," he said, "if you only grow up to be a noble, useful Christian woman, such as I hope one day to see you, I shall feel more than repaid for all the anxiety, care, and trouble of your training."

Chapter Tenth

$\mathscr{G}$uests and entertainers, old and young, went to church the next morning—riding, driving, or walking, as best suited the inclination of each.

In the afternoon there was the usual gathering of the house servants and field hands on the lawn near the veranda, where the family and guests were seated, and Mr. Dinsmore, Dr. Landreth, and Captain Raymond each gave them a little talk suited to the sacredness of the day and their needs as members of the fallen race of man.

The captain, standing before them with an open Bible in his hand, said, "My friends, I want to talk with you a little about some of the words spoken by the Apostle Paul when he was taking leave of the leaders of the church at Ephesus. He told them that he had been testifying both to the Jews and also to the Greeks repentance toward God and faith toward our Lord Jesus Christ. Now, what is meant by repentance toward God? It is a feeling of true sorrow for our sins against Him—and everything wrong we have done, or thought, or felt is a sin against God. And what is it to have faith toward our Lord Jesus Christ? To believe in Him as one abundantly able and willing to save us—to save us from sin, from the love of it, and the punishment due to us for it. We are all sinners; we have all come short of the glory of God, neglecting many things that we ought to have done and doing very many things that we ought not to have done. We are all born with a sinful nature, and God only can change it, so that we will hate sin and love holiness. He only can give us true faith in His dear Son the Lord Christ.

"'By grace are ye saved through faith; and that not of yourselves: it is the gift of God.' We are saved by grace. It is only of God's undeserved goodness, not because we have done or can do anything pleasing in His sight. Paul speaks in this same chapter of the Gospel of the grace of God. *Gospel* means good news, and what could be better news than that? That God offers us salvation of His free, unmerited grace? What an offer that is! Salvation as His free, undeserved gift without money and without price. His offer is, 'Come unto Me and be ye saved all ye ends of the earth.' No one is left out; this wonderful offer is to each one of us and to every other inhabitant of this world, so that if anyone fails to be saved, the fault will be all his own. For God has said, 'I have no pleasure in the death of him that dieth: wherefore turn yourselves and live ye.' And oh, how plain He has made it that He does love us and would have us live! 'For God so loved the world that He gave His only begotten Son, that whosoever believeth in Him should not perish, but have everlasting life.'"

The service was not a long one, and when it was over the captain repaired to the schoolroom with Lulu and Gracie to hear them recite their Bible verses and catechism.

When that duty had been attended to, "Now, daughters," he said, "if you have anything to say or question suitable to the sacredness of the day to ask, I am ready to listen and reply to the best of my ability. Even a child may ask a question that a grown person cannot answer," he added with a smile.

"Indeed, papa," said Gracie, putting an arm round his neck and laying her cheek lovingly to his. "I think you do know 'most everything, and I'm oh so glad God gave you to me for my own father."

"I know you are, Gracie, I'm sure of it. But you can't be gladder than I am that he is my father, too," said Lulu, lifting to his eyes full of both filial love and reverence.

"Nor than I am that these two little girls are my very own," responded the captain, holding both in a close embrace. "But now for the questions."

"I have one to ask, papa," said Lulu. "It is what does the Bible mean by growing in grace?"

"Growing in likeness to Jesus and in conforming to His will—having more and more of the love and fear of God in our hearts, more faith and patience, and more love to our fellow creatures—for the more we love the Master, the more we will love those whom He died to redeem."

"And the more we love Him, the more we will try to be like Him?" Lulu said in a tone of mingled assertion and inquiry.

"Yes, my child, and it is the dearest wish of my heart that I may see my children thus growing in grace and in likeness to the dear Master."

"Papa, I want to," said Gracie softly. "Oh, I want to, very much!"

"Then ask God to help you, my darling, always remembering that He is both the hearer and the answerer of prayer."

"And you will ask Him for both of us, won't you, papa?" asked the timid, little girl.

"I will; I do, my darling. There is never a day when I do not pray earnestly for each one of my dear children, that God will make them His own true followers and keep them in every time of trial and temptation, taking them safely to heaven at last. Life in this world is exceedingly short compared with the external existence that awaits us all in another—that life of infinite joy and blessedness at God's right hand, or of everlasting, untold misery and unending, inconceivable anguish in the blackness of darkness, shut out forever from His presence," he added in moved tones. "God in His infinite goodness and mercy grant that the first and not the last may be the portion of each one of my beloved children!"

"Oh, papa," said Gracie softly, "how can anyone help loving the dear Savior who died that we might go to heaven and not to that other awful place!"

"Oh," said Lulu, "I do want to love Him more and serve Him better! When I think of His wonderful goodness and love to us poor sinners, I'm just as ashamed as I can be that I don't love Him at all as I ought and that I am so often ill-tempered and selfish and bad. Papa, I do really think it is kind and good of you to punish me when I deserve it, and I need it to make me a better girl."

"I shall be very glad indeed if you never again make it necessary for me to do so," he responded.

"I do hope I won't," she returned. "Papa, I'm very much afraid I'll be thinking and talking today about the wedding and what everybody is going to wear at it, and I know I won't be in half so much danger of doing so if I keep close to you. So mayn't I?"

"Yes, my dear, eldest daughter. I am always glad to have you near me," he said kindly. "It pleases me that you are very desirous to avoid temptation to do wrong."

"And you are just as willing to let me keep near you, papa?" Gracie said inquiringly and with a wistful, pleading look up into his face.

"Certainly, my dear, little daughter. I love you not a whit less than I do your sister," he said, drawing her into a closer embrace. "However, you may both stay here reading your Bibles and Sunday school books for a half hour longer. Then I will come for you, and you may spend the rest of the day as close to your father's side as you choose." With that he left them.

"Such a dear, good father as ours is!" exclaimed Lulu, gazing after him with loving, admiring eyes.

"Yes, indeed! I am sure there couldn't be a better or dearer one. Oh, I do love him so!" said Gracie, turning over the leaves of her Bible. "Let's read verses then, Lu."

"I'm agreed, and let it be the book of Esther. I do think that is such a lovely story."

"So it is. And so is Ruth, and that's shorter. I don't believe we'll have time to read all of Esther before papa comes for us."

"Maybe not," assented Lulu. "We'll read Ruth."

They had finished the story and were talking it over when their father came. It was nearly teatime.

Sacred music filled up most of the evening, and all the young girls and boys retired early to bed that they might be ready for the pleasures and employments of the coming day. The older people sat somewhat longer upon the veranda, conversing upon topics suited to the sacredness of the day. They were Christians and loved to speak of the Master and the things concerning His kingdom.

"Then they that feared the Lord spake often one to another: and the Lord hearkened and heard it, and a book of remembrance was written before Him for them that feared the Lord and that thought upon His name. And they shall be Mine, said the Lord of hosts, in that day when I make up My jewels; and I will spare them as a man spareth his own son that serveth him."

As usual, Lulu was up early the next morning and joined her father in a walk under the trees along the bank of the bayou.

"Well, daughter, has the rest of the Sabbath made you ready for work in the schoolroom again?" he asked, smiling down affectionately into a face rosy, bright, and happy with health and merry spirits.

"Yes, papa, I feel more like it than I did on Saturday," she answered, lifting sparkling eyes, full of affection to his.

"I rejoice to hear it," he said. "It is by no means a pleasant task to me when I have to compel a pupil—one of my own children or the child of someone else—against his or her inclination. And I thoroughly enjoy teaching when all are happy and interested."

"As we all ought to be when we have such a kind, wise teacher, dear papa," she returned. "It will be difficult, very difficult, I'm afraid, to give my mind to lessons when we are all so much taken up with the preparations for the wedding, but I'm determined to try my very best to do so to please my dearest, kindest, best of fathers," lifting his hand to her lips.

"A father who would far rather be obeyed from love than fear," he said with a tender, loving look down into her face.

"Yes, I know you would, papa, and my love for you is, oh, ever so much stronger than my fear. Though I own I am afraid of your displeasure and punishments, for I know you can punish severely when you think it your duty and for my good. But I respect and love you, too, a great deal more than I would or could if you indulged me in bad behavior."

"I don't doubt it," he said. "And I, as I have often told you, punish you when I deem it needful, because I know you will be the happier in the end for being compelled to try to conquer your faults and happier than you ever could be if allowed to indulge them."

"Yes, papa, I know that is so. I am never at all happy when indulging wrong tempers and feelings," she acknowledged with another loving look up into his face.

At that moment they were joined in their walk by Evelyn and Rosie.

"Brother Levis," said Rosie, "you surely are not going to be unreasonable and tyrannical as to require lessons of us today?"

"I'm afraid I am, little sister," he replied with a smile. "And I hope you are not going to be so naughty and rebellious as to require any kind of discipline, are you?"

"I don't know," she said with a pretended pout. "I feel no inclination at all toward lessons, but a very strong one in favor of a ride or drive over to Magnolia Hall."

"Which can be gratified when both study and recitations have been duly attended to," returned the captain. "And if you are all in need of an escort, you may call upon me for that service."

"Oh, a thousand thanks! That will do very well indeed!" she exclaimed in a tone of relief and pleasure.

"And all the good and industrious little girls may go along," added the captain with a smiling look into Lulu's eagerly inquiring face.

"Thank you, papa. Thank you very much!" she exclaimed joyously. "I do want to go, and I intend to be as industrious as possible and as good and obedient, so that you can take me. And you'll take Gracie, too, if she wants to go, won't you?"

"Certainly," he said. "Gracie deserves all the indulgences and pleasures I can give her."

"You are very kind, indeed, captain, to spend so much of your time in teaching us today. I feel very sure you would enjoy going to Magnolia Hall with the other gentlemen and the ladies this morning," remarked Evelyn with a grateful, affectionate look up into his face.

"Thank you, my dear," he replied. "It would be pleasant to me to go, but it is also a pleasure to help my own children and other appreciative pupils to climb the hill of science."

Just then Gracie and little Elsie came running to meet them, and the next minute the breakfast bell summoned them all to the house.

After breakfast followed family worship, school, playtime, then dinner, and, late in the afternoon, the pleasant drive through the woods to Magnolia Hall. It was only for a call, however, and at teatime the Viamede family and all their guests gathered about the table there.

From then until the wedding day the young folks were in a state of pleasurable excitement, though the captain kept his pupils steadily at their work, and they found it not impossible to fix their minds upon their studies for a portion of each day. The other relatives invited had arrived, and in a few days the marriage was to take place.

It was Saturday morning. Scarcely two hours had been spent in the schoolroom when the captain dismissed his pupils, telling them with his pleasant smile, that they had done very well indeed and they would be allowed a holiday until the wedding festivities were over. This announcement no one was sorry to hear, although he had made the lessons as interesting and as enjoyable to them as ever since undertaking the work of teaching them. All returned warm thanks, and Rosie, Evelyn, and Walter hastened from the room, which Captain Raymond had already left; but his two little girls lingered there a while longer, putting their desks in perfect order.

"Gracie," said Lulu, "how much money do you have left?"

"Not a single cent," was the reply in a rather rueful tone. "And I suppose yours is all gone, too?"

"Yes, every cent of it. I feel as poor as a little church mouse."

"But we are not wanting to buy anything just now, and papa will be giving us some pocket money again pretty soon," returned Gracie in a determinedly cheerful tone.

"Yes, so he will! Oh, what a dear, good, kind father he is! I really don't believe there are many girls of our ages that get so much pocket money every week. And papa gave us so much extra money, too, to use in buying our wedding gifts for Cousin Betty."

"Oh, yes, and now I think of it, I don't believe we ought to expect any more pocket money for a good while. Do you, Lu?"

"No, I don't. This wedding's costing a good deal—to papa as well as other folks, and the journey home will cost ever so much, besides all that papa paid to bring us here. Then, too, he's going to see Max again after we get home, and he will maybe take one or both of us along—if we're good, Gracie."

"Oh, do you think so?" exclaimed Gracie. "Oh, I'd love to see Maxie! But if only one of us can go it ought to be you, because you're the oldest, so that it wouldn't give papa half so much trouble to take care of you as of me."

"I'm just sure papa doesn't think it any trouble to take care of you, Gracie," returned Lulu in her quick, earnest way. "And you are a better girl than I, therefore more deserving of such indulgences."

"That's a mistake of yours, Lu," said Gracie. "You've been good as gold ever since we came to Viamede—as well as before—and helped papa with your typewriter, while I haven't done anything but wait on him a little, try to learn my lessons well, and amuse the little ones sometimes."

Lulu's face had grown very red while Gracie was speaking, and she hung her head in a shamefaced, remorseful way.

"No, Gracie," she said in a low, mortified tone. "I haven't been half so good as you think. I displeased papa very much that day when you all went to Magnolia Hall, and I had to stay at home and learn my lessons over. I was very angry and cross with dear little Ned because he meddled with my herbarium, which I had carelessly left lying out on my desk. If papa had punished me very severely it would have been no more than I deserved, but all he did was to send me to my room for a while till I told him how sorry I was and asked forgiveness of him and Neddie, too."

Gracie looked surprised. "No, I never heard a word of it before," she said. "But I'm sure you did all you could when you asked forgiveness of both of them—papa and Neddie."

The little girls had no idea that their father was within hearing, yet such was the case, and their little talk pleased him greatly.

"The darlings!" he said to himself. "They shall not be long penniless, for their father thinks them very worthy to be trusted with pocket money. Two more unselfish children I am sure it would be hard to find."

With that he rose and went to the library, to which they presently followed him, asking if there was anything he wanted them to do.

"Why, it is your playtime, daughters," he returned with a loving smile into the two, bright, young faces.

"But we'd like to do something to help you, dear papa," Gracie said, laying her small, white hand on his arm and looking lovingly up into his face.

"Yes, indeed, we would, papa," said Lulu, standing on his other side and putting her arm round his neck. "Please, if you have letters to answer, mayn't I write them for you on my typewriter?"

"Does my eldest daughter deem that a privilege?" he asked, smiling down into her beseeching eyes, while he put one arm round her, the other about Gracie's waist, and drew both in between his knees, kissing first one and then the other.

"Indeed I do, papa," Lulu answered in an earnest tone. "It's very sweet to me to feel that I am of even a little use to my dear, dear father, who does so much for me, taking so much trouble to teach me, giving me so many, many nice things to eat, to wear, to read, and to amuse myself with—so many that it would take quite a long while to count them all up."

"Ah, that reminds me," he said, taking out his wallet, "I shouldn't wonder if my little girls had about emptied their purses in buying gifts for the bride that is to be and so forth. Get them out and let me see what can be done in the way of replenishing them."

He noted with pleasure that as he spoke, each young face grew very bright.

"We've left them upstairs, papa," said Lulu. "And though you're ever so kind," hugging and kissing him again, "we don't want to take any more now when you have to spend so very much on the wedding and to take us all home to Woodburn."

"No, indeed, we don't, you dear, dear papa," chimed in Gracie, nestling closer to him and patting his cheek lovingly.

"My precious little darlings!" he said, holding them close. "Your father can spare it without denying himself or anybody else anything at all needful, and he feels very sure that he could not get more enjoyment out of it in any other way. So get your purses and bring them here to me," he concluded, releasing them from his embrace.

They ran joyfully to do his bidding, and on their return each found a little pile of money waiting for her—two clean, fresh, one-dollar bills, two silver half dollars, four quarters, and ten dimes—all looking as if just issued from the mint.

"Oh! Oh! Oh!" they cried. "How much! And all so bright and new!" Lulu added. "Papa, are you quite, quite sure you can really spare all this without being embarrassed?"

"Yes, quite sure," he returned, regarding her with a twinkle of fun in his eyes. "I really think I should not be embarrassed if called upon for twice as much, Lulu."

At that Lulu drew a long breath of relief, while Gracie threw her arms about his neck, saying, "You dear, dear papa! I don't believe any other children ever had such a good, kind father as ours."

"Well, now, I really hope there are a great many other fathers quite as good and kind as yours," he said with a smile, pinching the round, rosy cheek, kissing the ruby lips, and fondly stroking the soft, shining curls of her pretty head.

"I hope so," said Lulu, "but I'm just sure there's not another one I could love so dearly as ours. I do think God was very good to me in making me yours, papa. Your very own little daughter."

"And me, too," said Gracie.

"Yes, good to me as well as to you," responded the captain. "My darlings seem to me the dearest, most lovable children in the world. Well, Lulu daughter, you may help me with your machine for an hour, if you wish."

"Oh, yes, papa. Yes, indeed! I'll be glad to!" she exclaimed, hastening to uncover it, put in the paper, and seat herself before it, while her father took up a letter, glanced over the contents, then began his dictation as her fingers plucked out a response.

It was a business note and had no interest for Gracie, who presently wandered out upon the veranda with her well-filled purse in her hand.

Grandma Elsie sat there alone, reading. "What a bright, happy face, my little Gracie," she said, glancing up from her book as the child drew near. "Has some special good come to you, dear?"

"Yes, ma'am. See!" exclaimed the little girl, displaying her well filled purse. "It was empty, and my dear papa has just filled it. You see, Grandma Elsie," drawing near and lowering her voice, "I was wanting to buy a few things for goodbye presents to some of the servants, but I'd spent every cent of my money and thought I'd have to give it up. I'm oh so glad that I won't have to now. And—oh, Grandma Elsie, you and mamma will help me to think what will be best to get for them, won't you?"

"I will be very glad to do anything I can to help you, dear child," replied Grandma Elsie in her low, sweet tones, softly stroking the golden curls as the little girl stood close at her side. "Suppose you get a pencil and paper from the schoolroom and make out a list of those to whom you wish to give a gift and opposite to each name the gift that seems most suitable."

Gracie's reply was a joyful assent, and she hurried away in search of the required articles.

She was not gone more than a very few minutes, but on her return she found that her Mamma Vi, Rosie, and Evelyn had joined Grandma Elsie on the veranda and had been told by her what was the business at hand. They all were desirous to have a share in it.

They had a pleasant time over their lists, each making out one for herself, while Lulu finished the work she had undertaken for her father. They decided to write to the city for what was wanted, and that anyone else who wished could send at the same time. So that matter was most pleasantly and satisfactorily disposed of.

"Oh!" exclaimed Gracie struck by a sudden thought. "Suppose I run to the library and tell papa and Lulu about it, get him to tell her what to say, and let her write on the typewriter for the things?"

Everyone thought it an excellent idea, and Gracie immediately carried it out.

"I quite approve," her father said, when she had told her story and made her request.

"I, too," said Lulu. "I'll join you if papa will help me decide what to buy. I'll write the letter, too, if he will tell me what to say."

"I am entirely willing to do both, daughter," he said. "Let us set to work at once, as it will soon be dinner time, and I want to take my little girls out for a drive this afternoon."

"Oh, thank you, papa. Thank you very much!" they cried in joyous tones.

"Is anybody else going, papa?" asked Lulu.

"Your Grandma Elsie, Mamma Vi, and our little ones, in our carriage and as many more as may wish to go either in other carriages or on horseback. Perhaps you would prefer to ride your pony?"

"Not if you are to be in the carriage," Lulu replied.

"Ah, you are very fond of being with your father," he said with a pleased smile.

"Yes, indeed, sir! Just as close as I can get," stroking and patting his cheek, then pressing her lips to it in an ardent kiss.

"And it's exactly the same with me, you dear, darling papa!" exclaimed Gracie, putting her arm round his neck. "And it's exactly the same with every one of your children from big Maxie down to baby Ned."

"I believe it is, and it makes me very happy to think so," he replied. "But now, my dears, we must get to work on our list of articles."

Chapter Eleventh

*I*t was a large party that set out from Viamede shortly after leaving the dinner table. Most of the young people—among them Chester, Frank, Maud, and Sydney Dinsmore, Evelyn Leland, Rosie and Walter Travilla—preferred riding.

These, having swifter steeds, presently distanced the rest of the riders, as well as those who were driving. In passing a plantation, which was the home of Nettie Vance, a schoolmate of the Viamede young folks at the time several years before of their attendance at Oakdale Academy, they were joined by her and a young man whom she introduced as her brother. They were both well mounted and looking merry and happy.

"Bob and I were just starting out for a ride," she said, "and consider ourselves fortunate in meeting with such good company. May I take my place alongside of you, Miss Leland? I have a bit of news to tell you that I think will interest you and Miss Travilla. It is that Signori Foresti, who, as you will doubtless remember, was a teacher of music at Oakdale Academy when we were there together, is quite ill—partly from an accident, partly from drink, and extremely poor. I must say I hardly pity him very much for that last, but I do feel sorry for his wife and children."

"I, too," said Evelyn. "I wish it were in my power to relieve them, but my purse is about empty at present. However, I will report the matter to Viamede, and I am sure the kind friends there will see that something is done immediately toward supplying their pressing needs."

"Yes," returned Nettie. "I have heard a great deal of the kindness and benevolence of Mrs. Travilla and her father and of Captain Raymond's also. Though I for one could hardly blame him if he utterly refused to give any assistance to a man who had abused his daughter as Foresti did Lulu."

"Nor I," said Evelyn. "Yet I feel almost certain that he will assist Foresti. He would not let the wife and children suffer for the man's ill deeds, nor indeed the man himself, unless I am greatly mistaken, for the captain is a truly Christian gentleman."

"Indeed he is," said Rosie. "He is benevolent and exceedingly kind to the poor or to anyone who is in distress of any kind. I am very proud of that brother-in-law of mine, Nettie, and I don't care who knows it."

"I do not wonder at that," returned Nettie. "I certainly should be if he were mine. It is very plain from the way in which Lulu and Gracie look at him that they are both fond and proud of their father."

"Nor do I wonder at it," said Robert Vance, joining in the conversation. "Nettie pointed him out to me at church last Sunday, and I remarked then that he was as fine-looking a man as ever I saw—tall, straight, handsome in features, and of a most noble countenance."

"Thank you," Rosie said with a smile and a bow. "I think him all that and as noble in character as in looks. It is my opinion that my sister Violet drew a prize in the matrimonial lottery and the captain also, for Vi is in every way worthy of him."

"Surely," returned the young man. "One glance at her is sufficient to assure one of that."

Rosie and Evelyn then asked where the Forestis were to be found, and what were their pressing needs. Having learned those particulars, they promised that someone from Viamede would call to see if they could relieve them, Rosie adding with a smile, "We, as you probably know, are busy with preparations for a wedding in the family, yet I have no doubt some one or more among us could find time to attend to this call for help."

"Yes," said Walter, who had been quietly listening to the talk, "mamma will be sure to find time for such an act of kindness. She always does."

"I am sure of it," responded Nettie heartily, "from her sweet looks and all I have heard of her. And so your cousin, Miss Johnson, is going to be married?" she added, looking at Rosie. "We received our invitations yesterday, and we are busy with our preparations. It must be delightful to have such a thing coming off in the family, particularly to be the bride. I hear it is to be quite a grand affair and the match an excellent one."

"Yes," returned Rosie, "we are all much pleased with what we have heard of the gentleman, and I hope they are going to be very happy together."

"I hope so, indeed," responded Nettie. "I am but slightly acquainted with Miss Johnson, but I have always liked her looks."

It was near teatime when the Viamede party reached home again, and the ladies and little girls had barely enough time to dress for the evening before the summons to the table.

It was while all were seated about it that Rosie and Evelyn told of the news learned from Nettie Vance in regard to Signor Foresti and his family.

"Ah, poor things! We must do something for them," Grandma Elsie said when the story was finished. "Papa, shall we stop there tomorrow on our way to or from church? It would be a work of mercy suited for the day, I think. Do not you?"

"Yes," replied Mr. Dinsmore. "And it might be well to carry a basket of provisions with us."

Lulu had listened in silence while the others were talking, and all through the evening she had but little to say, seeming much of the time lost in thought. Usually she was quite talkative, unless, as occasionally happened, she was checked by a slight reminder from her father that it would be more becoming in a child of her age to show herself a quiet listener to older people.

The captain noticed her abstraction, but guessing at the cause, said nothing about it till they were alone together in her bedroom. Then, drawing her to her usual spot on his knee, "My little girl has been unusually silent this evening," he said. "Is anything wrong with her?"

She drew a long sigh. "I have been trying to decide a question of duty, papa," she said. "And, please—I'd like you to tell me what to do."

"In regard to what, daughter?"

"Giving a part of my money—the money you put into my purse this morning—to—to—the Forestis."

"I think it would be right and kind for you to do so. Do you not?"

"Yes, sir, and I will do it," she said with sudden determination. "It will be returning good for evil, as the Bible bids us. Won't it, papa?"

"Yes, and I think it will help you to forgive the man for his ill treatment of you," drawing her closer and kissing her fondly.

"Yes, sir. Even the resolve has made me feel more kindly toward him. How much ought I to give, papa? I hardly think I'll have very much left after I've paid for the presents I've sent for—you remember, for the servants here."

"No, not a very great deal, I presume, but you are not likely to need much before there will be more pocket money coming to you."

"Oh, no, sir. I'll not want for a thing, of course, because my dear, dear father provides everything I need to eat or wear and pays my traveling expenses, too, so that I'm not really obliged to spend anything on myself," she said, putting an arm about his neck and laying her cheek lovingly to his. "Papa, do you think a dollar will be enough for me to give the Forestis?"

"You may decide that question yourself, my darling," he said, patting her cheek and stroking her hair. "I leave it entirely to you to give much, little, or nothing, as conscience and inclination dictate."

"Thank you, papa. You are very kind to say that, but please tell me if you think a dollar will be enough for me?"

"Yes, I do," was his reply, and Lulu looked quite satisfied and relieved.

"I'm glad, papa," she said. "For I really do not know that I shall have more than that left after paying for the presents for the servants, and, of course, I can't give more than I have."

"Quite true," he returned with a slight smile. "I would have you make it a rule never to go into debt for your own gratification or for any other object. 'Out of debt, out of danger,' is a very old and wise saying. Now, daughter, it is time to say good night, but first let me remind you that tomorrow is the Lord's day and to be kept holy. Try not to think of the exciting events expected in the coming week, but to spend the time in the worship of God and the study of His Word, that you may grow in grace and conformity to His will, thus becoming 'meet for the inheritance of the saints in light,' and ready, when He shall call you away from earth, to dwell forever with Him in that holy, happy land where sin and sorrow are unknown. We will kneel down together now for a moment and ask Him to help us both to do so, 'running with patience the race set before us, ever looking unto Jesus the author and finisher of our faith.'"

Sunday was passed by the Viamede family in the usual quiet way, most of its hours filled up with divine service in the sanctuary or at home, and all retired to rest at an early hour, to rise the next morning in renewed health and strength, the children rejoicing in their holiday and the near approach of the wedding festivities.

Mr. and Mrs. Dinsmore had the day before on their way to church called upon the Italian music teacher, taking with them delicacies for the sick man and other articles of food for the rest of the family. They provided some money also, in which was included Lulu's dollar and, finding the services of a physician were needed, had engaged to send one.

Dr. Dick Percival undertook the errand, made a professional call, and on his return reported that the man was quite ill, but likely to recover with good and competent nursing. He went over again on Monday morning, but he called first at Viamede to report to his Uncle Horace and the captain.

Lulu was present at the interview and heard with interest all that Cousin Dick had to tell about the *signor* and his family.

"There are three children," said Dick. "They are forlorn-looking little creatures with apparently no playthings except a few broken bits of china and some corn cobs wrapped in rags for doll babies."

"Oh, papa," exclaimed little Elsie, who was seated upon her father's knee, "mayn't I send dem some of my dollies?"

"Yes, if you want to do so," he replied, smiling upon her and smoothing her curls caressingly with his hand.

"And I will hunt up some playthings for them, too, if I may, papa," said Lulu.

"Certainly," he said. "You may do so at once, and we three and Gracie will drive over there in the carriage, which I will order immediately. That is, if Cousin Dick does not object to our company?"

"Not by any means, captain. I shall be delighted to have it," said Dr. Percival. "And will you drive over with me, Art?" turning to Dr. Conley.

"With pleasure, Dick," was the reply, and in a short time all were on their way—the children well laden with toys and sweets for the little Forestis."

Violet had been invited to accompany her husband, but she declined because of some preparation still to be made for the wedding. Little Ned, however, had no such excuse, and he gladly made one of the merry little party in his father's carriage.

Dr. Percival, having other patients needing his attention, said he intended to make but a short call upon the Italian, and the captain did not think it worth while for his children to alight. From the carriage they witnessed with delight the pleasure conferred upon the little Forestis by their gifts.

Captain Raymond left them for a few moments while he went in to see the sick man, to whom he spoke with the utmost kindness, condoling with him on his sufferings and inquiring if they were very great.

"De bains ish ver bad, sare," replied the man with a heavy sigh. Then, with an earnest look into the captain's face, his own flushing hotly, "You, sare, ish de fader off Mees Lu Raymond?" he inquired.

"I am, sir," replied the captain with a little sternness of look and tone.

"Mees Lu, she bees one goot leetle girl for senden me that monish yesterday," continued Foresti. "Dot make me ver sorry I haf so leetle batience mit her dat time she sthrike me mit de music book."

"Yes," said Captain Raymond, "and I trust that when you are again able to teach you will try to be more patient and forbearing with your pupils. It will be better for both you and them."

"Yes, sare, I will try dat blan, but mine batience bees sorely dried mit de mishtakes off dose careless bupils I haf to teach."

"I dare say that is true," said the captain. "Maybe, one who finds it impossible to have patience with pupils should try some other way of making a livelihood than by teaching."

In another minute or two the captain left, not waiting for the doctors, who were, as he knew, going in another direction, re-entered his carriage, and started on the return trip to Viamede.

"Papa," asked Lulu, "can we take a little different route going home?"

"Yes," he replied in an indulgent tone and gave the necessary directions to the driver.

It was a pleasant, shady road into which they presently turned, and the children chatted and laughed right merrily, receiving no rebuke from their father and fearing none.

They had not gone far on the road when they espied two horsemen quickly approaching from the opposite direction.

"Oh," cried little Elsie, "here come Cousin Ronald and Uncle Horace."

"An unexpected meeting, captain," the younger Mr. Dinsmore remarked with a bow and smile as they drew near.

"But none the less pleasant, Horace," returned Captain Raymond.

"Very true, sir," said Mr. Lilburn, bowing and smiling in his turn.

"For the captain and you young folks, no doubt, but a trifle less delightful for us who have the load to carry," seemed to come from the mouth of one of the horses, as he tossed his head to shake off a fly.

"True enough, Selim. You doubtless envy me with only this gentleman to carry, and I pity you from the bottom of my heart. Only, it must be good fun to hear those little folks chattering and laughing," was the answering remark apparently made by the horse ridden by Mr. Lilburn, speaking as they passed the captain's carriage.

Lulu and Gracie clapped their hands, laughing merrily, while baby Ned exclaimed with a look of astonishment, "Me didn't fink horsey could talk like udder folks!"

"Yes! But why did they never do it before?" cried little Elsie. "Papa, did you know they could talk?"

"I never heard them do so before, daughter," the captain said with an amused smile down into the earnest, surprised little face. "And I suspect that it is only when Cousin Ronald is about that they can."

Chapter Twelfth

Rides, drives, sports of various kinds, and preparations for the wedding made the time pass very rapidly and pleasantly to the young folks at Viamede, Magnolia Hall, and the parsonage until at length all was in readiness for the long-awaited festivities.

The ceremony was to be performed at the church, the Rev. Cyril Keith officiating, and to be immediately succeeded by a wedding breakfast on the lawn at Magnolia Hall. That was to be about noon, so it did not interfere with the usual morning meal and family devotions at Viamede.

When these had been attended to, the ladies and young girls scattered to their rooms to dress for the important occasion.

It had been arranged that Gracie Raymond and Rose Lacy were to act as flower girls dressed in white tarlatan, white hats trimmed with white ribbon, and each carrying a basket filled with white roses, white japonicas, and smilax. Rosie Travilla, Evelyn Leland, and Lulu Raymond dressed as had been planned at the first were to act as bridesmaids, while Lora Howard and Maud and Sydney Dinsmore were to be maids of honor dressed in white and carrying bouquets of white flowers.

Betty's own dress was a rich white silk trimmed with elegant and costly lace—a generous gift of her brother-in-law, Mr. Embury—and a tulle veil fastened at her head with a wreath of orange blossoms. Her bouquet was of bride roses and smilax. The Dinsmore and Howard cousins were to act as ushers and groomsmen.

All this had been satisfactorily arranged, and rehearsals gone through with several times at Magnolia Hall and Viamede—that each one might be perfect in his or her part. Otherwise timid, little Gracie could not have been induced to undertake her share in the ceremony.

When she and Lulu were dressed for the occasion, they went in search of their father to ask his opinion of their appearance and attire. He scanned each daintily-attired, graceful little figure with a look of proud, fond affection, clasping them in his arms and kissing them tenderly.

"My darlings look very sweet in their father's eyes," he said. "But do not be too proud of your appearance, for fathers are apt to see their own children through rose-colored glasses, and it is not very likely that you will attract particular attention among so many attendants upon the bride, who will doubtless be gazed upon more admiringly and critically than anyone else."

"I'm ever so glad of that, papa," Gracie said with a sigh of relief. "Because I don't like to be viewed with a critic's eye," she concluded with a merry, though slightly disturbed, little laugh.

"Well, dear child, just try to forget yourself, and I have no doubt everything will go right," he said, drawing both her and Lulu closer into his arms for a little more hugging and kissing.

That was interrupted by the entrance of their Mamma Vi, coming upon the same errand that had brought them.

"Will I do, my dear?" she asked with a bright, winsome smile.

"Ah, my Violet, my sweet and beautiful flower," he returned, regarding her with ardently admiring eyes, "I fear you will outshine the bride. You look very like one yourself, except that most becoming air of maturity—scarcely older and certainly not less beautiful than when you gave yourself to me."

"And accepted you in return. Deeds which I have never yet for a moment regretted," she said with a coquettish smile up into his face, for he had put his little girls gently aside and risen to take a critical survey of his young and beautiful wife.

"And never shall if in my power to prevent it, my love, my darling," he said low and tenderly, laying a hand upon her shoulder and bending down to press a fond kiss upon her lips.

They were in the library, whither the captain had gone after arraying himself for the wedding festival to wait for the ladies and damsels who were to go under his care.

"Ah, Brother Levis, I have caught you in the very act," laughed Rosie, dancing into the room, already in bridesmaid's attire, and looking but little less attractive than Violet herself.

"Ah! And what of that, little sister?" he asked. "Who has a better right than her husband to bestow caresses upon a beautiful and attractive woman?"

"Captain Raymond, being my teacher, you have an undoubted and just right to question me in the schoolroom," laughed Rosie with an arch look up into his face. "But—I don't know that he has here and now. Now, please let me have your candid opinion of my dress and appearance."

"You will do very well, little sister. There is no fault to be found with your appearance, so far as I can see," he answered in a non-committal tone and with a mischievous twinkle of fun in his eye.

At that Rosie pretended to pout. "You keep all your compliments for Vi," she said. "But—ah, here comes Eva, and I wonder if you can afford one to her. She is certainly worthy of it."

Evelyn did indeed look sweet and fair in a becoming white chip hat and her pretty dress of pale blue silk trimmed with lovely lace.

Rosie's own dress was a delicate pink; Lulu's canary color; and all of the same material.

"That she is, in my opinion, returned the captain, bestowing a fatherly caress upon the young orphan girl then offering the same to Rosie.

"Well, now, you are a nice brother—my big, big brother, you remember," she laughed. "So I won't repulse you. Help yourself, and let us have it over."

Just at that moment her mother came in dressed for the wedding in a beautiful, pearl-colored silk and point lace, a knot of white roses at her throat and in her belt, and her lovely and abundant golden brown hair simply and tastefully arranged.

"Mamma!" exclaimed Violet. "You are the most beautiful and tastefully attired one among us!"

"In the partial eyes of my daughter, Violet," was the smiling rejoinder. "But to me her youthful beauty far exceeds her mother's fading charms.

"My opinion is that the fading is perceptible to no eyes but your own," remarked the captain gallantly.

"I, also," said Violet. "A richer, riper bloom is all that I can see."

"Or that anybody else can," added Walter, who, ready dressed for the wedding, had entered the room just in time to catch Violet's first exclamation.

Then the other members of the family and the guests came flocking in, the carriages were announced as waiting for their living freight, and presently all were seated in them and on their way to the church, which they found crowded with invited guests and other spectators.

The ceremony was short, but impressive. Bride, bridesmaids, flower girls, and maids of honor were all looking their best and behaved admirably. Groom, groomsmen, and ushers also looked their best, among whom were a brother and an intimate friend of the bridegroom, the young cousins Arthur and Walter Howard, Chester and Frank Dinsmore, and little Walter Travilla.

Old Mr. Dinsmore, the uncle and guardian of the bride, gave her away, and he was the first to salute, call her by her new name on the completion of the ceremony, to congratulate the groom, and to wish them a great deal of happiness.

Affectionate greetings and best wishes followed in quick succession, carriages were re-entered, and all drove to Magnolia Hall to partake of the wedding breakfast.

The place was looking its very loveliest. The grass on the lawn like a velvet carpet of emerald green, spangled with many flowers of varied hues, which filled the air with delicious perfume, and there, scattered about underneath the magnolia, orange, and other beautiful shade trees, were many small tables resplendent with the finest napery, shining silver, cut glass, and delicate china—all loaded with delicate and delicious viands.

Presently every table was surrounded by a merry group quite disposed to do justice to the tempting fare, and the air was filled with the pleasant hum of happy voices and low, gleeful laughter.

The bride and groom with their attendants were seated about two tables not many feet apart, while the older members of the Viamede family and Cousin Ronald occupied another quite near to both. Mr. Embury and his Molly with the parsonage family, Virginia, and the older Embury children filled a third—not far from either of the others. Presently, Nero, a great big Newfoundland dog belonging to Mr. Embury, showed himself at his master's side, looking up wistfully into his face.

"I'm hungry, good master," were the words that seemed to come from his lips, "and surely your faithful dog might have a taste of this feast."

At that some of the guests looked startled and astounded, too much surprised to speak, but Mr. Embury, who was not ignorant of Cousin Ronald's talents, though a little startled at first, recovered his wits instantly and replied, "Certainly, certainly, Nero. That's only fair." He handed the dog a generous bit of chicken and bade him carry it to a distance and eat it. An order which was promptly obeyed.

"Ah ha, ah ha, um h'm! That's quite a bright and capable dog, Mr. Embury," remarked Cousin Ronald, elevating his eyebrows in mock surprise. "What would you take for him, sir?"

"He is not for sale, Mr. Lilburn," was Mr. Embury's grave rejoinder. "You must surely see for yourself, sir, that he is no ordinary dog, but an uncommonly valuable animal. There are not many of his race who can speak so plainly."

"Ah ha, ah ha, um h'm! That is very true, sir. I don't wonder you are not inclined to part with him, for it is no easy matter to find a dog that can speak such good English, nor for that matter any other language, Mr. Embury."

"No, sir, they are scarce indeed," said Mr. Embury. "I had no idea Nero was one of them until he spoke just now."

"Ah, I'm afraid the power of speech will be lost by him as suddenly as it was found," remarked Mrs. Embury with a low, gleeful laugh.

"There must certainly be a ventriloquist among us," remarked the groom with a searching look at Cousin Ronald.

"Ah, do you really think so, sir?" inquired Mr. Lilburn gravely. "Would you do me the favor to point him out?"

"Well, sir, I cannot say that I am absolutely certain, but I am strongly inclined to the opinion that he sits in the chair occupied by yourself."

"Indeed, sir, I didna think I filled the place so ill that room could be found in it for another mon!" exclaimed Mr. Lilburn, again raising his eyebrows like one astonished, sending a downward glance over his own portly person, and assuming so comical an expression of countenance that no one could see it without smiling or laughing outright.

So fully was he absorbing the attention of all that no one noticed the return of Nero until words were again heard apparently issuing from his lips.

"That was a nice morsel, master, but not enough to satisfy the appetite of a dog of my size. Another bit, sir, if you please."

"Yes, sir, you shall have it, since you ask so politely," returned Mr. Embury, handing him another and larger piece of the chicken. "But carry it off where there will be no danger of contact with wedding finery."

Nero obeyed, and as he trotted away, a voice that seemed to come from behind Mr. Embury said whiningly, "I'm hungry, too, sir, and surely a human creature should be treated at least as well as a dog."

At that, Mr. Embury turned suddenly round as if to see the speaker, nearly everyone else doing likewise, but no beggar was in sight.

"Well, sir," he said, "I cannot give to an invisible suppliant. Show yourself if you want anything."

"Sir," replied the voice, now seeming to come from a clump of bushes near at hand. "I'm not used to begging, and I don't want to be seen. Can you not send a servant here with a plateful of your most toothsome viands?"

"Quite a modest request, sir," returned Mr. Embury, laughing. "But I think you will have to wait till the servants have more leisure. At present they are fully occupied in waiting upon my guests."

"But then you'll let him have something to eat, won't you, papa?" pleaded little Mary Embury. "You never do turn anybody away hungry."

"Certainly not, little daughter. If he could be found, he should be fed."

"But shan't I drive him out, sir?" queried a servant man. "We doan' want no beggars 'bout yar. Dey mout help deirselfs to some o' de silvah when nobody aint lookin'."

"Well, Bill, you might drive him out. Perhaps he is a tramp just watching for his opportunity to help himself."

Bill, well pleased with the errand, set down with alacrity the dish he carried and hurried toward the clump of bushes that apparently concealed the tramp. "Ki, you ole tief you!" he cried. "Git long out ob dis; nobody doan want yo' hyar! Be gone now, putty quick!"

He pulled apart the bushes as he spoke, but instantly he started back in astonishment and terror, as he perceived that no one was concealed there.

"Whar dat fellah dun gone?" he exclaimed. "Dis chile doan' see nobody dar nohow 'tall!"

"Ha, ha! You don't look in the right place," cried the same voice that had begged for food a moment before, the speaker seeming to be directly behind him. Bill wheeled about with unusual alacrity with the intention of seizing his tormentor, but he turned almost white with terror on perceiving that no one was there.

"Wha—wha—wha dat raskil done gone?" he exclaimed. "T'ot he right dar, an' he aint 'bout."

"Never mind, Bill. It seems he has saved you the trouble of driving him off," said Mr. Embury. "And you may come back to your duties. More coffee is wanted here."

Bill obeyed, but on his return with the coffee, he kept glancing quite apprehensively in the direction of the bushes.

"I wonder where the man did go!" exclaimed little Mary presently. "I've been watching, and I don't know how he could get away without being seen."

"Beggars are sometimes very quick at hiding, my little lassie," remarked Mr. Lilburn.

"Ha, ha! So they are!" cried the voice of the beggar once again, sounding as though he stood just behind her chair.

"Oh!" she exclaimed with a start and a backward glance. "Why, where is he? I don't see him at all."

"Don't be frightened, daughter," Mr. Embury said in an encouraging tone.

"No, bit lassie, he's not dangerous," remarked Mr. Lilburn with a reassuring smile.

"Oh, do you know him, sir?" she asked, looking up inquiringly into his face.

"I didna see him," replied the old gentleman laughingly. "But judging by his voice I think I know who he is—a quiet, inoffensive countrymon o' me ain, lassie."

"Ah, yes, a rather intimate acquaintance of yours, sir, is he not?" queried Norton with a searching look into the face of the old gentleman and a half-mocking smile.

"I think I may have heard the voice before, sir," Mr. Lilburn replied with unmoved countenance. "It is not unusual for beggars to accost one who is by no means o' the same class as themselves. In fact, as ony body can see, it would be useless to ask alms o' those no richer than themselves."

"Ah, true enough, sir!" was the reply.

Meanwhile, many mirthful glances had been exchanged by those—particularly the young folks—acquainted with the secret of Cousin Ronald's peculiar talent, and the guests at more distant tables were looking with a good deal of curiosity. Bill was presently questioned as he passed them on his way to and from the kitchen.

"What was it you saw yonder in that bush, Bill?"

"Nothin' 'tall, sah."

"But you seemed frightened. You looked scared."

"Dat's de reason, sah. Somebody talkin' an' nobody dare."

"Why, how's that, Bill?" queried another voice.

"Dunno, sah."

Questions were put to Mr. and Mrs. Embury and others as the guests drew together again upon the conclusion of the meal, but no satisfactory answers were elicited.

A reception occupied some hours after that, then all returned to their homes to meet again at Viamede in the evening, where a beautiful and bountiful entertainment awaited them.

The next evening a smaller party was given at the parsonage, and on the following afternoon the bride and groom took their departure for a little trip northward, expecting to settle down in their own home upon their return.

Chapter Thirteenth

$\mathcal{I}$t was only the next day after the departure of Betty and her husband that a letter was received by Mrs. Cyril Keith, informing her of the death of her Aunt Delaford, who had left the bulk of her large fortune to her and a fat legacy to each of the Conly brothers—Calhoun, Arthur, Walter, and Ralph and the sisters Virginia and Ella.

Isadore was well satisfied with the provisions of the will, as were the others also with the exception of Virginia, who frowned and grumbled audibly that she herself might have been made to share equally with Isadore, who had a good home and husband already, therefore really needed less than herself, "alone and forlorn and poor as a church mouse."

"But you have no children, Virgie," said her Cousin Elsie in whose presence the remark was made. "You've no one to support but yourself, and the interest of this money will be sufficient for your comfortable maintenance."

"Possibly, if I had a home, as Isa has, but not without," returned Virginia in a peevish tone, while her eyes flashed angrily.

Elsie bore patiently with the rebuff and said no more at the time, but she considered the matter earnestly, carefully, and prayerfully in the privacy of her own room, then had a talk about it with her father, without whose approval she seldom took a step of any great importance.

Finding him alone on the veranda, "Papa," she said, taking a seat by his side, "I want a few minutes' chat with you before we are joined by anyone else. You heard Virginia's complaint of yesterday—that she had no home of her own. I have been thinking it over and also of the fact that Dick and Bob are in the same condition, and it has occurred to me that I might invite them to take possession here while we are absent at our more northern home, giving employment to the servants, keeping the house in repair and the grounds in order. That is, they could merely oversee the work and look to me for the means necessary to cover the expenses. I would retain my present satisfactory overseer and pay his wages and those of the laborers out of the returns from the crops."

"You mean that you would simply give a home here to your cousins?" asked Mr. Dinsmore.

"Yes, sir, a home without expense—except, perhaps, some small increase of the wages of the servants in consideration of the additional work made for them and a share of the fruits, vegetables, fowls, and so forth raised upon the plantation."

"A share? Meaning all they might want to use? The 'and so forth' I suppose, meaning milk, cream, butter, and eggs?"

"Yes, sir."

"I should call it a very generous offer, and I have no objection to bring forward, seeing that you are well able to afford it, if it is your pleasure to do so."

"I am glad my project meets with your approval," she said with a smile. "For otherwise, as I think you know, papa, it would never be carried out. Ah, how thankful I should be, and I hope I am, that I have been given the financial ability to do such kindness to others!"

"Yes," he said with an affectionate smile into the soft, hazel eyes looking into his. "I know of no one who enjoys doing kindness more than my dear, eldest daughter.

"What a delightful winter and early spring we have had here," he continued after a pause. "But it is now growing so warm that I think we must soon be moving northward."

"Yes, sir. When the last arrivals have had a week or more of the enjoyment to be found in this lovely region of the country."

"Yes. They are enjoying it," he said with a pleased smile. "The younger ones especially—the children of your brother and sister not less than the others. By the way, daughter, I think you will be doing no little kindness to your cousins Cyril and Isadore by giving Virginia a home here."

"Yes, I think their home life will be more peaceful," she said in assent. "Poor Virgie seems to be not of—the happiest or most contented disposition."

"No, she never was," said Mr. Dinsmore. "Quite a discontented, fretful, complaining creature she has always been since I have known her, and she was a very little child when our acquaintance began."

In the course of that day Elsie's plans were made known to the Keiths, Virginia, Dick Percival, and his half-brother Bob Johnson, which was joyfully accepted by the two gentlemen, half ungraciously so by Virginia, who said complainingly, that, "Viamede was a pretty enough place, to be sure, but would be dreadfully lonesome for her when the boys were away."

"Then you can amuse yourself with a book from the library, a ride or drive, as the horses and carriages will be left here for your use and that of Dick and Bob," Elsie answered pleasantly, while

Isadore, blushing vividly for her sister, exclaimed, "Oh, Virgie, you could not have a lovelier, sweeter home, and I think Cousin Elsie is wonderfully kind to offer it!"

"Of course, I'm greatly obliged to her," Virginia said, coloring slightly as though a trifle ashamed of her want of appreciation of the kind offer. "And I'll not damage anything, so that the house will be none the worse for my occupancy, but possibly a little better."

"Yes, perhaps it may," Elsie said pleasantly. "The servants usually left in charge are careful about airing it and keeping everything neat and clean. I really think you will have no trouble whatever with your housekeeping, Virgie."

"That seems a pleasant prospect, for I never liked housekeeping," returned Virginia. "I really am much obliged to you, Cousin Elsie."

"You are very welcome, and I hope you will be happy here," was the kindly reply.

Another fortnight of constant interchange between Viamede, Magnolia Hall, and the parsonage of visits, rides, drives, walks, sailing, rowing out on the lagoon, and every other pleasure and entertainment that could be devised ensued. Then the party began to break up, those from the north returning to their homes, most of them by rail, as the speediest and the most convenient mode of travel. However, Mr. and Mrs. Dinsmore, Evelyn, Grandma Elsie and her youngest two, Cousin Ronald, and the Woodburn family returned together by sea, making use of the captain's yacht, which he had ordered to be sent to him in season for the trip by the Gulf and ocean.

There was no urgent need of haste in their travels, and the captain did not deny that he was conscious of a longing to be, for a time again, in command of a vessel sailing over the briny deep. Besides, it would be less fatiguing for the little ones, to say nothing of their elders.

The little girls were full of delight at the prospect of both the voyage and the return to their lovely homes, yet they could not leave beautiful Viamede without deep regret.

It was the last evening but one of their stay. All were gathered upon the veranda, looking out upon the lagoon sparkling in the moonlight and the velvety flower-bespangled lawn with its many grand and beautiful old trees. The little ones had already gone to their nests, but Evelyn, Lulu, and Gracie were sitting with the older people—Gracie on her father's knee, the other two together close at hand.

There had been some cheerful chat followed by a silence of several minutes. It was broken by a slight scuffing sound, as of footsteps in the rear of Elsie's chair, then a voice said in mournful accents, "'Scuse de in'truption, missus, but dis chile want to 'spress to you uns dat we uns all a'most heartbroke t'inkin' how you's gwine 'way an' p'r'aps won't be comin' heah no mo' till de ol'est ob us done gone foreber out dis wicked worl'."

Before the sentence was completed every eye had turned in the direction of the sounds, but nothing was to be seen of the speaker.

"Oh, that was you, Cousin Ronald," laughed Rosie, recovering from the momentary start given her by the mysterious disappearance of the speaker.

"Ah, Rosie, my bonnie lassie, how can you treat your auld kinsman so ill as to suspect him?" queried the old gentleman in hurt, indignant tones.

"Because, my poor abused cousin, I am utterly unable to account in any other way for the phenomenon of an invisible speaker so close at hand."

Cousin Ronald made no reply, for at that instant there came a sound of bitter sobbing, apparently from behind a tree a few feet from the veranda's edge, then a wailing cry, "Oh, Miss Elsie, Massa

Dinsmore, and de res' ob you dar, doan' go for to leab dis po' chile! She cayn't stan' it nohow 'tall! Her ole heart like to break! Doan' go way, massa an' missus. Stay hyah wid dese uns dat lubs you so!"

"Oh, Cousin Ronald, don't!" Elsie said in half tremulous tones. "It seems too real, and it almost breaks my heart, for I am greatly attached to many of these old men and women."

"Then I think they will not distress you with any more complaints and entreaties tonight, sweet cousin," returned the old gentleman in pleasant, though half-regretful tones.

Chapter Fourteenth

The next day the servants were gathered on the lawn and presented with the parting gifts procured for them by the ladies and little girls, which they received with many thanks and demonstrations of delight. But the following morning, when the time of parting had really come, there were some tears shed by the old retainers, yet they were greatly cheered by the assurances of their loved mistress, her father, and Captain Raymond that in all probability it would not be very long before the family would be there again for a season.

The feelings of the departing ones were of mingled character—regret at leaving lovely Viamede and joy in the prospect of soon being again in their own sweet homes farther north.

The weather was delightful, as light, fleecy clouds tempered the heat of the sun. The fields and plantations were clothed in the richest verdure of spring; the air was filled with the perfume of flowers and vocal with the songs of birds; and upon reaching Bayou Teche, they found their own yacht, the *Dolphin*, awaiting them.

The young folks of the party greeted her with a clapping of hands and many other demonstrations of delight. Soon all were onboard, and she was steaming out through the bay into the Gulf beyond—her passengers, from Grandpa Dinsmore down to baby Ned, grouped together on deck underneath an awning.

"We are in the Gulf now, aren't we, sir?" asked Walter at length, addressing the captain.

"Yes, my boy," was the pleasant-toned reply. "Are there any places along its coast that you or any others would particularly like to see?"

"Oh, yes, sir. Yes, indeed!" exclaimed Walter with enthusiasm. "I for one would like greatly to see Mobile Bay with its fort. Morgan is the name?"

"Yes. Fort Morgan is at the extremity of Mobile Point, where Fort Bowyer stood in the War of 1812. You remember what happened there at that time?"

"It was attacked by the British, wasn't it, sir?"

"Yes, in September of 1814 by a British squadron of two brigs and two sloops of war aided by a land force of 130 marines and six hundred Indians led by the Captain Woodbine, who had been trying to drill them at Pensacola.

"Florida did not belong to us at that time. The Spaniards had made a settlement at Pensacola in 1696, and they were still there at the time of our last war with England. They favored the British, who organized there, as well as in other parts of Florida, expeditions against the United States. The Spanish governor, though professing neutrality, evidently siding and giving the British aid and comfort."

"And when then did we get possession of Florida, sir?" asked Walter.

"In July of 1821," answered the captain.

"Didn't Jackson capture Pensacola at one time during that war with England?" asked Evelyn.

"Yes, in the attack about which Walter was just asking, before Lafitte forwarded to New Orleans those documents showing how the British were trying to get him into their service. Jackson had perceived that the Spaniards were, as I have said, secretly siding with the British, and now, with the positive proof furnished by those papers before him, he squarely accused Manrequez, the Spanish governor of Pensacola, of bad faith.

"Then followed a spicy correspondence, which Jackson closed by writing to the governor, 'In future I beg you to withhold your insulting charges against my government for one more inclined to listen to slander than I am; nor consider me any more a diplomatic character unless so proclaimed from the mouth of my cannon.'

"Then he set to work to raise troops, and in a very short time, he had two thousand sturdy young Tennesseeans ready for the field.

"But before these reached Mobile, hostilities had begun. Jackson himself went there early in August, and on his arrival he perceived that an attempt would be made by the British to seize it as soon as the talked-of great expedition should be ready to move.

"Fort Bowyer was only a very small and weak fortification. She had no bomb-proofs and but twenty guns, only two of them larger than twelve-pounders, some still smaller in size.

"Yet small and weak as was the fort, it was the chief defense of Mobile. So Jackson threw into it 130 of his Second Regular Infantry under Major William Lawrence, who was as gallant an officer as any in the service.

"Lawrence at once made every preparation in his power to resist the expected attack. But before he could complete his work on the morning of the twelfth of September, the British Lieutenant-colonel Nichols appeared on the peninsula behind the fort with, as I have said, his marines and Indians—the latter under the command of Captain Woodbine, who had been drilling them at Pensacola.

"Later in the evening of the same day the four British vessels of which I spoke appeared in sight and anchored within six miles of Mobile Point. They were a part of a squadron of nine vessels in Pensacola Bay under the command of Captain Percy.

"Our little garrison slept upon their arms that night. The next morning Nichols caused a howitzer to be dragged to a sheltered point within seven hundred yards of the fort and threw some shells and solid shot from it but without doing much damage to the fort."

"And our fellows fired back at him, of course?" exclaimed Walter excitedly.

"Yes, but their fire was equally harmless. Later in the day, Lawrence's guns quickly dispersed some of Percy's men who were attempting to cast up entrenchments and in the same way several light boats, whose men were engaged in sounding the channel nearest the fort.

"The next day was occupied in very much the same way, but on the third the garrison perceived that an assault was to be made from both land and water. At two o'clock the vessels were seen approaching, and Lawrence called an immediate council of officers.

"All were determined to resist to the last, and if finally compelled to surrender, to do so only on condition that officers and privates should retain their arms and private property, be treated as prisoners of war, and protected from the Indians.

"The words adopted as the signal for the day were, 'don't give up the fort.'

"At half-past four the battle began, the four vessels opening fire simultaneously and pouring broadside after broadside upon the fort, which returned a fearful fire from its circular battery.

"While this was going on in front, Captain Woodbine was assailing our men in the rear from behind his sand dune with a howitzer and a twelve-pounder.

"So the battle raged for an hour; then the flag of the *Hermes* was shot away, and Lawrence stopped firing to learn if she had surrendered. But the *Caron* fired another broadside, and the fight went on with renewed vigor. Soon a shot cut the cable of the

Hermes, and she floated away with the current, her head toward the fort and her decks swept of men and everything by a raking fire from the fort.

"Then the fort's flagstaff was shot away, and her ensign fell, but the British, instead of following Lawrence's humane example, redoubled their fire. At the same time, Woodbine, supposing that the fort had surrendered, hastened toward it with his Indians, but they were driven back by a storm of grape-shot, and almost immediately the flag was seen again floating over the fort at the end of the staff to which Major Lawrence had nailed it."

"Was that the end of the fight, papa?" asked Lulu.

"Very nearly, if not quite," he replied. "Two of the attacking vessels presently withdrew, leaving the helpless *Hermes* behind. She finally grounded upon a sandbank, when Percy fired and abandoned her. Near midnight her magazine exploded."

"I should think that was a great victory. Was it not, Brother Levis?" queried Walter.

"I think it was," the captain said. "The result was very mortifying to the British. It was entirely unexpected, and Percy had said that he would allow the garrison only twenty minutes to capitulate. It was not surprising that he expected to take the weak little fort with its feeble garrison of 130, when he brought against it over thirteen hundred men and ninety-two pieces of artillery.

"The Americans lost only eight men, one half of whom were killed. The assailants lost 232, 162 of them killed.

"One result of that fight was that the Indians lost faith in the invincibility of the British, and many of them deserted and sought safety from the anger of Jackson by concealing themselves in the interior of their broad country."

"Papa," said Gracie earnestly, "did not God help our cause because we were in the right?"

"No doubt of it, daughter," replied the captain. "Ours was a righteous cause—a resistance to intolerable oppression and wrong, as our poor sailors felt it to be when a British man-of-war would stop our merchantmen on the high seas and force into their service any man whom they choose to say was an Englishman.

"But I need not enlarge upon that subject to my present audience, as I am convinced that you all know of and appreciate that bitter wrong.

"To resume. The Americans were highly gratified with the result of the conflict at Fort Bowyer, and their zeal was greatly quickened for volunteering for the defense of New Orleans, whose citizens testified their appreciation of Major Lawrence's achievement by resolving to present him with an elegant sword in the name of their city."

"Was there not a second attack by the British upon Fort Bowyer, captain?" asked Evelyn.

"Yes, after their defeat at New Orleans. That, you will remember, was on the eighth of January, 1815. They reached the fleet, lying in the deep water between Ship and Cat Islands, on the twenty-ninth of that month, Fort Bowyer on the ninth of February, and besieged it for nearly two days, when Major Lawrence found himself compelled to surrender to a superior force. That left Mobile at the mercy of the foe, but just then the news of peace concluded at Ghent nearly two months before reached them."

"But wasn't there some fighting done there or at Mobile in the Civil War, sir?" asked Walter.

"Yes, on August 5, 1864, the government forces under Farragut attacked the Confederate defenses there, consisting principally of the two forts—Morgan on the eastern side of the bay and Gaines on the western—about three miles apart.

"A line of piles and a double one of torpedoes stretched nearly across from Fort Gaines to Fort Morgan, leaving only a narrow channel between that fort and the point of termination. It was through that channel, indicated by a red buoy, that blockade runners passed in and out. Inside of these defenses lay the Confederate ironclad *Tennessee,* and three wooden gunboats. It was early in the morning of that August day that Farragut's signal was given for the advance of his seven sloops of war. The firing was heavy and destructive on both sides. But I will not go into particulars at this time, only saying that the result was in favor of the Federals. But the victory cost many lives—of Federals 335 men, of whom 113 were drowned in the Tecumseh. She was the leading monitor, which had struck a torpedo and gone down. Fifty-two of the Federals were killed by shot, while the Confederate loss was ten killed, sixteen wounded, and 280 prisoner, besides the loss in the forts, which is unknown."

Just at that point a passing vessel attracted the attention of the captain and his listeners, and the conversation was not renewed until after dinner.

Chapter Fifteenth

*I*t was Mrs. Travilla, or Grandma Elsie, who that afternoon started the captain upon the historical sketches so greatly enjoyed by the younger part of the company, to say nothing of the older ones.

"We will pass near enough Fort Gaines and Morgan to get a view of them—the outside at least—will we not, Captain?" she asked with her usual sweet smile.

"Yes, mother," he replied. "Pensacola also, whither, as I have said, the British went after their fruitless attack upon Fort Bowyer—now Fort Morgan—which was then occupied by the Spaniards under Manrequez and where they were publicly received as friends and allies.

"All that and the revelations of Lafitte concerning their attempt to engage him and his outlaws to help them in their contemplated attack upon New Orleans kindled the hottest indignation in the minds of Jackson and the people. The general issued a proclamation in retort for one sent by the British officer Nichols shortly before, in which he had made inflammatory appeals to the French, who were prejudiced against the Americans, and the Kentuckians, who were discontented because of a seeming neglect by their government. This state of things largely owed to the arts of ambitious politicians.

"Nichols had also sent out Indian runners to excite their fellows against the Americans, and in that way he gathered nearly a thousand Creeks and Seminoles at Pensacola, where they were supplied with an abundance of arms and ammunition.

"Jackson in his proclamation told of all this, the conduct of the British, and the perfidy of the Spaniards and called upon the people of Louisiana to 'arouse for the defense of their threatened country.'"

"And did they do it, sir?" queried Walter.

"Yes. They were thoroughly roused and much excited by the threatening aspect of affairs, and at once they set vigorously to work to prepare for determined resistance to the threatened invasion of their country and their homes.

"Jackson was impatient to march on Pensacola and break up that rendezvous of the enemies of the United States, but it was slow work to get his troops together, and November had come before he had his forces ready for the attack.

"At last, however, he had four thousand men gathered at Fort Montgomery, due north of Pensacola, and on the third of the month they marched for that place, some Mississippi dragoons leading the way.

"On the evening of the sixth, Jackson with his whole army encamped within two miles of their destination. Major Pierre was sent to the Spanish governor with a flag of truce and a message from his general saying that he had not come to injure the town or make war upon a neutral power but to deprive the enemies of the republic of a place of refuge. Pierre was also to demand the surrender of the forts.

"The British, however, were in possession of Fort St. Michael, over which theirs and the Spanish flag had been waving together until the day before, and as soon as the American flag of truce was seen approaching, it was fired upon from the fort by a twelve-pounder.

"Pierre returned to Jackson and reported these facts. Then Jackson sent to the governor a Spaniard whom he had captured on the way, demanding an immediate explanation.

"The governor asserted that he knew nothing of the outrage and promised that another flag should be respected.

"At midnight Pierre, sent again by Jackson, called once more upon the governor with a proposal that American garrisons should be allowed to take possession of the forts until Manrequez could man them with a sufficient number of Spanish troops to enable him to maintain the neutrality of his government against violations of it by the British, who had taken possession of the fortresses, it seemed, in spite of the Spanish governor's protests. The American troops were to be withdrawn as soon as the additional Spanish ones arrived.

"The governor rejected the propositions and before dawn three thousand of the Americans were marching upon Pensacola. They passed along the beach, but the sand was so deep that they could not drag their cannon through it. Then the center of their column charged gallantly into town, but on reaching the principal street, they were met by a shower of musketry from the gardens and houses, while a two-gun battery opened upon them with balls and grape-shot.

"But Captain Laval and his company charged and captured the battery when the governor quickly showed himself with a flag and promised to comply with any terms offered if Jackson would spare the town."

"I hope Jackson wasn't too good to him after all of that," laughed Rosie.

"The surrender of all the forts was what Jackson demanded and received," replied the captain. "But one, six miles away, called Fort Barancas, commanding the harbor in which the British vessels lay, was still in the hands of the enemy. Jackson determined to march suddenly upon it the next morning, seize it, turn its guns on the British vessels, and capture or injure them before they could escape.

"But before morning the British squadron had gone, carrying with it Colonel Nichols, Captain Woodbine, the Spanish commandant of the fort, and about four hundred men, besides a considerable number of Indians. Before leaving, they had blown up the fort.

"Jackson suspected that they had gone to make another attack upon Fort Bowyer and the town of Mobile, so he hurried away in that direction, leaving Manrequez angry and indignant at this treatment of himself by the British and the Indians filled with the idea that it would be very imprudent for them to again defy the wrath of Andrew Jackson. Much dejected and alarmed, the Indians scattered themselves through the forests.

"As for Jackson, when he reached Mobile on the eleventh of November, he received messages urging him to hasten to the defense of New Orleans.

"He left that place on the twenty-first and reached New Orleans on the second of December—but of what he accomplished there I have already told you in our previous discussions of New Orleans and the surrounding areas."

"Yes, papa," said Lulu. "I'll never forget that interesting story. But do tell me, will we pass near enough to Mobile to see those forts?"

"Yes," he said. Then turning to Grandma Elsie, the captain asked, "Mother, would you like to stop and visit the forts?"

"I am willing if the rest wish it," she replied. "But otherwise I would prefer to press on toward home, my Ion home, which, now that we have left Viamede fairly behind, I begin to long to see again."

"That being the case I am sure no one of us will wish to stop," returned the captain gallantly, a sentiment at once echoed by Mr. Dinsmore and all present.

"We are nearing there now, are we not, my dear?" asked Violet.

"Yes. We are moving rapidly, and if all goes well, we may expect to see the forts early this evening."

There was an exclamation of pleasure from several of the young people. Then Lulu asked, "Papa, are there not some other historical places we shall have to pass while we are in the Gulf or after we reach the ocean?"

"Quite a number, daughter, but we will not delay our voyage in order to visit them at this time."

"Perhaps some other day, then?" she returned inquiringly, smiling up into his face as she spoke.

"Very possibly," he returned, smoothing her hair with his hand. She was, as usual, close at his side.

A pause in the talk was at length broken by a remark from Cousin Ronald.

"You had some great men among your Union officers, captain, in both army and navy in the days of that terrible Civil War."

"We had indeed, sir," was the hearty response. "A number of them in both arms of the service, and none more worthy of respect and admiration than Farragut, who did such splendid service at both New Orleans and Mobile Bay, to say nothing of other places. The city of Mobile could not be captured as New Orleans had been, by reason of shoal water and obstructions in the channel, but the passage of blockade runners, carrying supplies to the Confederacy, was stopped, which was the main object of the expedition."

"Yes, he did good service to his country," returned Mr. Lilburn. "Although, if I mistake not, he was a southerner."

"He was born in Tennessee," replied Captain Raymond. "In the winter of 1860–61 he was waiting orders at Norfolk, Virginia, where he watched with intense interest the movements of the southern states and especially the effort to carry Virginia out of the Union into the Confederacy. When that was accomplished, he remarked that 'the state had been dragooned out of the Union.'

"He talked freely on the subject and was told that a person with such sentiments as his 'could not live in Norfolk.' 'Well, then,' he replied, 'I can live somewhere else,' and that very evening left the place with his wife and son. That was the eighteenth of April of 1861. He went first to Baltimore, but afterward he took a cottage at Hastings on the Hudson.

"The next December he was summoned to Washington, and on the second of February he sailed from Hampton Roads for New Orleans."

"Where he certainly did splendid service," remarked Mr. Lilburn. "I hope it was appreciated."

"I think she did," returned the captain. "He received many marks of the people's appreciation, among them a purse of $50,000, which was presented to him for the purchase of a new home in New York City."

"Did he live to see the end of the war, sir?" asked Walter.

Yes. He was on the James River with General Gordon when Richmond was taken, and on hearing the news, the two rode there post-haste, reaching the city a little ahead of President Lincoln. A few days after that the naval and military officers at Norfolk with some of the citizens who had remained true to the Union gave the president a public reception.

"Farragut was one of the speakers and in the course of his remarks said, 'This meeting recalls to me the most momentous events of my life, when I listened in this place till the small hours of the morning, and returned home with the feeling that Virginia was safe and firm in her place in the Union. Our Union members of the convention were elected by an overwhelming majority, and we believed that everything was right. Judge, then, of our astonishment in finding, a few days later, that the state had been voted out by a miserable minority, for want of firmness and resolution on the part of those whom we trusted to represent us there, and that Virginia had been dragooned out of the Union. I was told by a brother officer that the state had seceded, and that I must either resign and turn traitor to the government which had supported me from childhood, or I must leave this place.

"'Thank God, I was not long in making my decision. I have spent half my life in revolutionary countries, and I know the horrors of civil war; and I told the people what I had seen and what they would experience. They laughed at me and called me "granny" and "croaker"; and I said, "I cannot live here, and will seek some other place where I can live." I suppose they said I left my country for my country's good, and I thank God I did.'"

"A countryman to certainly be proud of," remarked Mr. Lilburn.

"Oh, I wish I could have seen him!" exclaimed Gracie. "Papa, wasn't he a Christian man?"

"I think so, daughter," replied the captain. "He is said to have had a strong religious nature and a firm reliance upon providence, believing in God's constant guidance."

"Do you remember," said Grandma Elsie, "those lines of Oliver Wendell Holmes' written in honor of Admiral Farragut and read at a dinner given for him in which this passage occurs?

"Fast, fast are lessening in the light
The names of high renown,
VanTromp's proud besom pales from sight,
Old Benbow's half hull down.
Scarce one tall frigate walks the sea,
Or skirts the safer shores,
Of all that bore to victory
Our stout old commodores.
Hull, Bainbridge, Porter—where are they?
The answering billows roll,
Still bright in memory's sunset ray,
God rest each gallant soul!

A brighter name must dim their light,
With more than noontide ray:
The Viking of the river fight,
The Conqueror of the bay.
I give the name that fits him best—
Ay, better than his own—
The Sea-King of the sovereign West,
Who made his mast a throne."

"A fine poem indeed and with a subject worthy of all its praise," remarked Cousin Ronald, as Mrs. Travilla ceased. "No wonder you are proud of him, cousins, for he was, as I said a moment since, one to be proud of. I should be proud indeed of him were he a countryman of mine."

"As each one of us—his countrymen and women—certainly is," said Mr. Dinsmore.

There was a silence of a few moments, presently broken by the captain.

"Yes," he said, "I think there are few, if any, of his countrymen, who are not proud of our grand naval hero, Farragut. And there were others among our naval heroes of that day, almost, if not quite, as worthy of our affectionate admiration. Admiral Bailey, for instance, who was second in command at the taking of New Orleans, leading in the *Cayuga* the right column of the fleet of government vessels in the passage of Forts St. Philip and Jackson and ensuring the capture of the Chalmette batteries and the city.

"As you probably remember, he passed up ahead of the fleet, through the fire of the forts, the Confederates, vessels, the rams, fire-rafts, blazing cotton bales, and dense clouds of smoke, meeting the attacks of all unaided.

"Also it was he who was sent by Farragut in company with only one other man, Lieutenant George H. Perkins, to demand the surrender of the city, the taking down of the Confederate flag, and the hoisting in its stead of the Stars and Stripes.

"It certainly required no small amount of courage to pass through those city streets surrounded by a hooting, yelling, cursing crowd, threatening them with drawn pistols and other weapons.

"And who can fail to admire the words of Bailey in his official report of the victory, 'It was a contest of iron hearts in wooden ships against iron-clads with iron beaks—and the iron hearts won'?

"And not less admirable was his modest behavior at a dinner given him at the Astor House, when called upon to reply to the toast of 'The Navy.'"

"Ah, what was that, sir?" asked Mr. Lilburn, pricking up his ears.

"I was reading an account of it only the other day," pursued Captain Raymond. "The old hero straightened himself up and began, 'Mr. President and gentlemen—them—than ye.' Then he made a long pause, glancing up and down the table. 'Well, I suppose you want to hear about that New Orleans affair?' he continued. At that there were cries of 'Yes, yes!' and a great stamping of feet. So Bailey went on, 'Well, d'ye see, this was the way of it. We were lying down the river below the forts, and Farragut, he—he signaled us to go in and take 'em. Being as we were already hove short, it didn't take much time to get under way, so that wasn't so much of a job as ye seem to think. And then the engineers, they ran the ships, so all we had to do was to blaze away when we got up to the forts, and take 'em, according to orders. That's just all there was about it.' And he sat down amid thunders of great applause."

"Ah ha, um h'm, ah ha! A nice modest fellow he must have been," remarked Cousin Ronald, nodding reflectively, over his cane.

The call to tea interrupted the conversation, but on leaving the table they all gathered upon the deck to watch the sunset, the rising of the moon, and for the Forts Morgan and Gaines, upon which they all gazed with interest as the captain pointed them out and the vessel steamed slowly past.

"Ah, what a terrible thing is war!" sighed Grandma Elsie. "God forbid that this land should ever again be visited with that fearful scourge!"

"Ah, I can say amen to that!" Mrs. Dinsmore exclaimed, low and tremulously, thinking of the dear younger brothers who had fallen victims in that unnatural strife. "We cannot be thankful enough for the peace and prosperity that now bless our native land."

"No. May it ever continue," added her husband. "Her growth and prosperity since that fearful struggle ended have been something wonderful."

A few moments of silence followed, the vessel moving swiftly on her way and a gentle breeze fanning the cheeks of her passengers as they sat there placidly gazing out over the moonlit waters. The quiet was suddenly broken in upon by a loud guffaw followed by a drunken shout.

"Ain't I fooled ye nice, now? Ye didn't know I was aboard, cap'n, nor any o' the rest o' ye. Ye didn't guess ye'd got a free passenger aboard 'sides that old Scotch feller a-settin' yonder alooking like he feels hisself as good 's any o' the rest, ef he don't pay nothin' fer his trip."

Everybody started and turned in the direction of the sounds.

"A stowaway!" exclaimed Captain Raymond. "The voice seems to come from the hold. Excuse me, ladies and gentlemen. I must see to his case and that we are secured from the danger of a visit from him, as he is evidently a drunken wretch." And with the words he hastened away in the direction of the sounds.

"Ha, Ha! I hear ye, cap'n!" shouted the voice. "But drunken wretch or not, I wouldn't harm a hair o' yer heads. All I'm awantin' is a free passage up furder north, where I come from."

"Oh, mamma, I'm so frightened! I'm so 'fraid the bad man will hurt my dear papa," cried little Elsie, clinging to her mother, while tears filled her sweet blue eyes.

"No, papa will whip de naughty mans," said Ned, shaking his little baby fist in the direction of the sounds.

"Ah ha, ah ha, um h'm, little laddie. I have no doubt your papa is bigger and stronger than the naughty mans," said Cousin Ronald. "And if he catches the good-for-nothing scamp, he can whip him within an inch of his life."

At that Walter burst into a laugh. "Now, Cousin Ronald," he said, "I'd not be a bit surprised to learn that you are well acquainted with that scamp. However, I'll run after Brother Levis to see the fun, if there is any, but I'm sure nobody need be one bit afraid." And with that, away he ran.

"Ah, Cousin Ronald," began Violet, laughing and the others joining in with her. They were all entirely occupied in looking at the old gentleman, whose face, however, could be but indistinctly seen, as he had so placed himself that the moonlight did not fall fully upon it. She continued, "Confess that—"

But she got no further. A loud shout of drunken laughter from the other side of the vessel again startled them.

"Ha! The cap'n has gone in the wrong direction to catch this customer. But he needn't hunt me up. I'm a real harmless kind o' chap, an' I wouldn't hurt a hair o' any o' your heads."

Again every head was turned in the direction of the sounds. But seeing no one, they all burst into gleeful laughter, in which the captain presently joined, having returned from his bootless search, fully convinced that it need be carried no further.

Chapter Sixteenth

*I*t was a bright, sweet May morning. Reveille sounded at the Naval Academy at Annapolis, and with the very first tap of the drum Max woke and sprang from his bed. He glanced from the window as he hurried on his clothes, and a low exclamation of surprise and delight burst from his lips.

"What now, Raymond?" queried Hunt, who was dressing with equal expedition.

"The *Dolphin*!" cried Max in an exultant tone. "She lies at anchor there, and I haven't a doubt that I shall see my father and all the rest presently."

"Possible? What a fortunate fellow you are, Raymond," returned Hunt, hurrying to the window to take a peep. "Sure enough! What a beauty she is, that *Dolphin*! The captain will be here presently getting you leave to spend the day onboard, and it being Saturday, and he and the commandant old friends, there'll be no trouble managing it. Accept my most hearty congratulations, old fellow."

"Thank you," said Max, vainly trying to suppress his excitement, for his affectionate, boyish heart was bounding with joy at the thought of presently seeing his loved ones—most of all the father who was to him the personification of all that was good, honorable, brave, noble, and true; the father to whom, he knew beyond a doubt, he himself was an object of strong parental affection and pride.

"And it's fortunate for you that I'm the fellow to set the room to rights on this memorable occasion," continued Hunt. "I say, Raymond, I think you must have been born under a lucky star."

"Yes, old fellow," laughed Max. "I rather suspect that's it. But, hark! What's that?" as approaching footsteps were heard in the hall without.

A rap quickly followed. Max flew to the door and threw it open to find a messenger there from the commandant requiring his presence immediately in the grounds below.

Little doubting what awaited him, Max obeyed the summons with joyful alacrity, running down one flight of stairs after another till the lowest hall was reached, then out into the grounds, sending an eagerly inquiring look from side to side.

Ah, yes, in the shade of the tree yonder, a few yards from the doorway, stood the commandant in earnest conversation with another gentleman, not in uniform, but of decidedly soldierly bearing. Max recognized the face and form on the instant and flew to meet him.

Both turned at the sound of approaching footsteps.

Max hastily saluted his superior officer, saying half breathlessly, "I am here, sir."

"So I see, Raymond," was the smiling rejoinder. "For the present I resign you to this gentleman's care," turning toward the captain.

Max's hand was instantly clasped in that of his father, who held it fast and, bending down, kissed his son with ardent affection and said with emotion and in low, earnest tones, "My boy, my dear, dear boy!"

"Papa, papa!" cried Max, his voice, too, trembling with feeling and excitement, "I never was more glad in my life!"

"I am glad for you, Max," said the commandant in kindly tones. "And Raymond, let me assure you that the lad is worthy of every indulgence that could be afforded him—a more industrious or better behaved cadet I have never had under my care. Hoping to see you again in the course of the day, I bid you good morning. You also, Max," and with a bow and a smile, he left father and son alone together.

"So good a report of his son makes your father a very happy man, Max," the captain said, pressing the hand he held and gazing into the rosy, boyish face with eyes brimful of fatherly love and pride.

"Thank you for saying it, papa," returned Max, flushing with joy. "But with such a father I ought to be a better and brighter boy than I am. But I do try, papa, and I mean always to try to honor you by being and doing all I know you would wish."

"I haven't a doubt of it, my son," the captain said, again affectionately pressing the lad's hand then letting it go. "But now I must return to the *Dolphin*, taking my eldest son with me if he wishes me to do so."

"Yes, indeed, papa!" cried the boy, ready to dance with delight. "But may I go back to my room for a moment first? I'm afraid that in my hurry to obey the summons of the commandant, I haven't left everything quite in ship shape."

"Yes, go, son," replied his father. "And if your morning devotions have not been attended to, do not neglect them any longer. I will wait for you here under the trees. By the way, I am to hear your recitations for this morning, so you may bring the needed books with you."

"Yes, sir," returned Max and hurried away, his father looking after him with proudly beaming eyes till the lithe, graceful young figure disappeared within the doorway. Then taking a morning paper from his pocket, he seated himself on a bench beneath a tree to await the lad's return.

He had not long to wait. In a few minutes Max was again at his side, and the two were wending their way toward the rowboat that was to take them to the *Dolphin*, anchored some distance out in the stream.

All was so still and quiet in and about the vessel that morning that her passengers slept later than usual, but Lulu, as generally happened, was one of the earliest risers and had not been up long before she hastened to the deck to exchange the accustomed morning greeting with her father. But, to her surprise and disappointment, a hasty glance about the deck showed her that he was not there.

"Why, what's the matter?" she said to herself. "I'm afraid papa must be sick, for I do not know what else would keep him in his stateroom till this time of day. But," with another sweeping glance from side to side, "we're certainly anchored, and where? Why it looks like—yes, it is Annapolis!" hearing the splash of oars and catching sight of a rowboat with several persons in it, "Oh, there's papa and Max with him. Oh, oh, oh, how glad I am!" With those words she ran to the side of the vessel, and the next minute was in Max's arms.

It was a hearty embrace on the part of both, their father standing by and watching their embrace with shining eyes.

"Oh, Maxie, how you have grown!" exclaimed Lulu, gently withdrawing herself from his embrace and scanning him with keen scrutiny from head to foot. " You look every inch a naval cadet."

"Do I?" he queried laughing. "Thank you, for I consider it a decided compliment. And you, too, have changed. You are taller, and you look more than ever like papa."

"Oh, Max, you could not say anything that would please me better than that," she exclaimed, flushing with pleasure. "And I can return the compliment with interest. I think you will look exactly like our dear father when you are his age," turning toward the captain and lifting her eyes to his full of ardent filial affection. He was standing there regarding both with fatherly tenderness and pride in their youthful comeliness of form and feature.

"My dear, dear children!" he said, bending down to give Lulu the usual morning caress, "your mutual love makes me very happy. May it never be less than it is now!"

At that moment Violet, Gracie, and the two little ones joined them, and more hearty, loving embraces followed, all, except Violet, being as much taken by surprise at the sight of Max as Lulu had been.

Gracie almost cried with joy as Max caught her in his arms and hugged her close, kissing her sweet lips again and again.

"I doubt," he said laughingly, as he let her go, "if there is another fellow at the Academy who has such sisters as mine, or such a young, pretty mamma, or darling baby brother and sister," kissing each in turn. "And," looking up into his father's face, a telltale moisture gathering in his eyes, "I'm perfectly certain there's not one can show a father to be so proud of."

"Ah, my dear boy, love is blind to defects and very keen-sighted as regards good and admirable qualities in those she favors," was the captain's answering remark.

"What a surprise you have given us, papa!" exclaimed Lulu. "To me at least, for I hadn't the least idea we were coming here."

"No, but some of the rest of us knew," said Violet with a merry little laugh. "Your father told me of his intentions last night—as a secret, however, for he wanted to give you and Gracie a pleasant surprise."

"And it was certainly a pleasant one to me," said Max. "Papa, thank you ever so much."

"Did you get leave for him to stay all day, papa?" asked Lulu i tone that seemed to say she hoped so with all her heart.

"He will be with us through the day, except during the two hours of drill, which we will all go to see and also all day tomorrow," was the captain's reply to that, and it seemed to give pleasure to all who heard it. All the passengers onboard were well pleased, for by that time the others had come up to the deck, and one after another gave Max a hearty greeting—the older people as one they had expected to see, the younger ones with joyful surprise. They all gathered about him, some of them—Walter especially—with many, many questions in regard to the daily routine of life at the Naval Academy, all of which Max answered readily and to the best of his ability.

"Haven't you lessons to say today, Max?" queried Walter.

"Yes, but I'm to recite them to papa," Max replied with a pleased, smiling glance up into his father's face.

"You may well look pleased, Max, for he's an excellent teacher, as all of his Viamede pupils can testify," remarked Rosie demurely.

"Oh, yes, I remember now that he has been teaching you all while you were down there," said Max. "Well, I never saw a better teacher, though, perhaps, being his son and very fond of him, it's possible I may be a partial judge."

"Quite possible, my boy," laughed his father. "And I think no one of my pupils is disposed to view me with a critic's eye."

"You need not say the rest of it, papa," said Lulu, "for I'm sure you haven't any imperfections to be passed by."

"Quite right, Lu," laughed Violet.

At that moment came the call to breakfast—a summons everyone was ready to obey with alacrity. They had a pleasant, social time about the table; the fare was excellent, appetites were of the best, and everyone was in fine spirits and a high, good humor.

Max was called upon to answer so many questions with regard ɔ life at the Academy, and his replies were listened to with so much ʿerence, that the captain began to fear his boy might become ʿferably conceited. Disturbed by that fear, he watched him so closely and with so grave an air that at length Max noticed it. He was much disturbed with the fear that he had unwittingly done or said something to hurt or displease his dearly loved father.

He took the first opportunity—following the captain about the vessel after breakfast and family prayers were over, till they found themselves alone together for a moment—to inquire, in a tone of much concern, if it were so.

"No, my son, not at all," was the kindly reply. "But I felt a little anxious lest my boy should be spoiled and made conceited by being applied to by older people for so much information."

"I hope not, papa. I know very well it was only because I've been living there and they haven't, and that every one of them knows far more than I do about many another thing."

"Quite true, my son," the captain said with a smile, adding, "and now you may get out your books and look over those lessons, as I shall soon be ready to hear them."

"Yes, sir. It will be a really great treat to recite to my old tutor once more," returned the lad with a look of relief and pleasure. "I am very glad indeed that he is not displeased with me as I feared."

"Very far from it, my dear boy," was the captain's kindly rejoinder. "The account given me today by the commandant of your conduct and attention to your studies was most gratifying to my pride in my eldest son."

Those words and also warm praise bestowed upon his recitations when they had been heard filled the boy's heart with happiness. His father returned to the Academy with him at the hour for drill, but the others witnessed it from the deck of the *Dolphin*. At its conclusion, Captain Raymond and his son returned to the yacht, Max having permission to remain there until nearly ten o'clock on Sunday night.

A trip up the river was planned for the afternoon, anchor was weighed, and the yacht started as soon as her commander and his son had come aboard.

All were seated upon the deck under an awning, greatly enjoying a delicious breeze, the dancing and sparkling water, and the distant view of the shore arrayed in the lovely verdure of spring.

Mrs. Dinsmore, Mrs. Travilla, and Mrs. Raymond sat together, busy with fancy work and chatting cheerily, while the younger ones had their drawing materials or books—except Gracie, who was dressing a doll for little Elsie. Few of them, however, were accomplishing a great deal, there being so small necessity for the employment and so many things to withdraw their attention from it.

Max speedily made his way to Mrs. Travilla's side. She looked up from her work and greeted him with her sweet smile. "It is quite delightful to have you among us again, my dear boy," she said, taking his hand and pressing it affectionately in hers.

"Thank you, dear Grandma Elsie," he returned, his eyes sparkling. "It is a great pleasure to hear you say so, though I don't know how to believe that you can enjoy it half so much as I do."

"I am glad to hear that you do, laddie," she said brightly. "Suppose we have a bit of chat together. Take that chair here and tell me how you enjoy that artillery exercise you have just been going through."

"Thank you, ma'am," said Max laughingly, as he took the seat indicated. "It's really delightful to be treated as a relative by so dear and sweet a lady, but you do look so young that it seems almost ridiculous for a great fellow like me to call you grandma."

"Does it? Why, your father calls me mother, and to be so related to him surely must make me your grandmother, Max."

"But you are not really old enough to be his mother, and I am his oldest child."

"And you begin to feel yourself something of a man, since you are not called Max, but Mr. Raymond at the Academy yonder?" she returned in a playfully interrogative tone.

Max seemed to consider a moment, then smiling, but blushing vividly, "I'm afraid I must plead guilty to that charge, Grandma Elsie," he said with some hesitation.

"What is that, Max?" asked his father, drawing near just in time to catch the last words.

"That I begin to feel that—as if I'm a—at least almost—a man, sir," answered the lad, stammering and coloring with mortification.

"Ah, that's not so very bad, my boy," laughed his father. "I believe that at your age I was more certain of being one than you are—really feeling rather more fully convinced of my own wisdom and consequence than I am now."

"Were you indeed, papa? Then there is hope for me," returned the lad with a pleased look. "I was really afraid you would think me most abominably conceited."

"No, dear boy, none of us think you that," said Mrs. Travilla, again smiling sweetly upon him. "But you have not yet answered my query as to how you enjoyed the artillery exercise we have just seen you go through."

"Oh, I like it!" returned Max, his eyes sparkling. "And I don't think I shall ever regret my choice of profession if I succeed in passing and become as good an officer as my father has been," looking up into the captain's face with a smile full of affection and proud appreciation.

"Now I fear my boy is talking of something he knows very little about," said the captain, a twinkle of fun in his eye. "Who told you, Max, that your father had been a good officer?"

"My commandant, sir, who knows all about it, or at least I think he does."

At that instant there was a sound like the splashing of oars the farther side of the vessel, and a boyish voice called out, "A there, Raymond! A message from the commandant!"

"Oh, I hope it isn't to call you back, Maxie!" exclaimed Lulu, springing up and following Max and her father as they hastened to that side of the vessel, expecting to see a rowboat there with a messenger from the Academy.

But no boat of that kind was in sight. Could it have passed around the vessel? Max hurried to the other side to make sure, but no boat was there.

"Oh!" he exclaimed with a merry laugh. "It was Mr. Lilburn," and he turned a smiling amused face toward the old gentleman, who had followed and now stood close to his side.

"Eh, laddie! What was Mr. Lilburn?" queried the accused. "That I'm no' down there in a boat is surely evident to all who can see me standing here. Are ye no' ashamed to so falsely accuse an auld friend who wad never do harm to you or yours?"

Then a voice seemed to come from a distant part of the vessel. "Ah, sir, ye ken that ye're known to be up to such tricks. All only to make fun for your friends, though, not to cause fright or harm to anyone—unless it be a gambler or some other rascal."

"Hear that, will you now, cousin!" cried Mr. Lilburn. "Somebody seems ready to do justice to the auld man our fine young cadet here is so ready to suspect and accuse."

By this time all the other passengers had joined them on that side of the vessel, everybody but the very little ones understood the grand joke, and it was received by all onboard with merry peals of laughter.

To Max, the afternoon and evening seemed to pass very quickly, so delightful was it to be once more surrounded by dear ones, not the least pleasant part being a half hour spent alone with his father after the others had retired. He had so many little confidences that would not willingly have shared with anyone else, and they were with so much evident interest, such hearty sympathy, and they were replied to with good and kindly advice. Max was even more firmly convinced than ever before that such another dear, kind, and lovable father as his was nowhere to be found.

And the captain was almost equally sure that no other man had a son quite so bright, handsome, intelligent, noble, industrious, and in every way worthy to be the pride of his father's heart, as this dear lad who was his own.

"God, even the God of his fathers, keep my dear boy in every hour of trial and temptation, and help him to walk steadily in the strait and narrow way that leads to everlasting life," he said with emotion when bidding his son good night. "Keep close to the dear Master, my son, ever striving to serve and honor Him in all your words and ways, and all will be well with you at the last."

Chapter Seventeenth

The captain, Max, and Lulu were all three early on deck the next morning—as lovely a May morning as ever was seen. The sun had but just showed his face above the horizon when Lulu mounted the companionway to the deck, but she found her father and brother already there, sitting side by side, both looking very happy and content.

"Good morning, papa and Max," she said, hurrying toward them.

The salutation was returned by both in cheery, pleasant tones.

"I thought I'd be the very first on deck, but here you both are before me," she added as she gained her father's side.

"But pleased to have you join us," he said, drawing her to a seat upon his knee. "A sweet Sabbath morning, is it not? How did my little girl sleep?"

"As well as possible, papa. It is much cooler here than at Viame now, and a delightful breeze came in at the window. But I al always sleep well, and that is something to be thankful for, is

"It is, indeed," he responded. "May my dear, eldest daughter never be kept awake by the reproaches of a guilty conscience, cares, anxieties, or physical distress—though that last I can hardly hope she will escape always until she reaches that blessed land where 'the inhabitants shall not say, I am sick.'"

"Yes, sir," she said. "I ought to be very thankful that I am so healthy. I hope I am, but any kind of physical pain I have ever been tried with is far easier for me to bear than the reproaches of a guilty conscience. I can never forget how hard they were to endure after I had hurt little Elsie so because I was in a passion."

"I can't bear to think of that time," said Max. "So let us talk of something else. The view out here is lovely, is it not, papa?"

"Oh," cried Lu in surprise, "we are at anchor again in the river at Annapolis, aren't we, papa?"

"Yes. I brought you all back here in the night to spend the Sabbath. I think we will go into the city to church this morning, and we shall have some religious exercises on the vessel this evening."

"Oh, I like that plan," said Max, "especially the afternoon part, for I am really hungry for one of those interesting Bible lessons with you for my teacher."

"Yes, Maxie, I pity you that you can't share them with Gracie and me every Sunday," said Lulu. "Papa, won't you give us—Max and Gracie and me—a private Bible lesson all to ourselves after the service for the grown folks, sailors, and all has been held—just as you used to do when we were all at home at Woodburn?"

"Quite willingly, if my children wish it. Indeed, it is what I had contemplated doing," replied the captain. "For we cannot better employ the hours of the holy Sabbath than in the study of God's Word, which He has given us to be a 'lamp to our feet and a light our path' that we may journey safely to that happy land where sin sorrow are unknown.

ver forget, my children, that we are but strangers and upon this earth, only passing through it on our way to an eternal home of either everlasting blessedness or never-ending woe—a home where all is holiness, joy, peace, and love, or to that other world of unending remorse and anguish, 'the blackness of darkness forever.'"

"It is very difficult to keep that always in mind, papa," said Max. "I hope you will often ask God to help us—me especially—to remember it constantly, and live, not for time, but for eternity."

"I do, my dear boy. There is never a day when I do not ask my heavenly Father to guard and guide each one of my dear children and give them a home with Him at last. But we must all strive to enter in at the strait gate, remembering the warning of Jesus, 'Strait is the gate, and narrow is the way, which leadeth unto life, and few there be that find it.'"

Violet joined them at that moment, then the rest of the party, one after another. Then came the call to breakfast, and soon after leaving the table and the holding of the regular morning service on the vessel, nearly everyone went ashore and to church.

At the close of the exercises, they returned to the *Dolphin*, dined, a little later assembled under the awning on the deck, and were presently joined by the greater part of the crew. Another short service, consisting of the reading of Scriptures, prayer, and the singing of hymns, followed.

After that, the captain took his three older children aside and gave them, as in the dear old times at Woodburn, a Bible lesson, in which they were free to ask of him as many questions as they would.

"Papa," said Gracie, "I was reading in Isaiah this morning this verse, 'Therefore, thus saith the Lord God, "Behold I lay in Zion for a foundation, a stone, a tried stone, a precious cornerstone, a sure foundation."' Does it mean the dear Lord Jesus, papa?"

"Yes, daughter. In both the Old and New Testament, Christ Jesus is called a Foundation. The foundation of a building is the part that supports all the rest, and Jesus is that to all His church, His people. He is the foundation of all the comforts, hopes, and happiness of the Christian; the foundation of the covenant God has made with His church; the foundation of all the sweet and precious promises of God's Word; a sure foundation on which His people may securely rest, knowing that He will never deceive, fail, or forsake anyone who trusts in Him. He is the only Savior, the head of the church, the only Mediator between God and man.

"We are not to look too much to our feelings, doings, prayers, or even our faith, but on the finished work of Christ. We can have assurance of hope, but we must attain to it by resting upon God's word of promise, remembering that it is Christ's righteousness which God accepts, not ours, so imperfect, so unworthy of mention.

"In that way only can we have peace and safety, for our own righteousness is but as filthy rags, exceedingly offensive in the sight of God, who is 'of purer eyes than to behold sin, and cannot look upon iniquity,' so utterly abhorrent is it to His holy nature.

"The Bible tells us, 'He that believeth on the Son hath everlasting life; he that believeth not the Son shall not see life; but the wrath of God abideth on him.'"

"Papa," said Gracie feelingly, "those are dreadful words, 'the wrath of God abideth on him.'"

"They are indeed," he said. "The one great question is, 'Do you believe on the Son of God?' There in Egypt, when God sent those plagues upon Pharaoh and his people, it was not the feelings of the Israelites that saved them, but the blood on the door posts, symbolizing the blood of Christ, which would in future ages be offered to satisfy the demands of God's broken law. And it was when he saw the blood that the angel passed over, harming them not.

"The scapegoat, too, was a symbol of Christ—bearing the sins of the people away into the wilderness. If our sins are laid on Jesus they will come no more to remembrance before our righteous Judge, but they will be covered with the beautiful robe of His righteousness. God will treat us as if it were our very own. Ah, my beloved children, it is the dearest wish of your father's heart that each one of you may have that righteousness put upon you!"

A slight pause and then Gracie said in low, clear, and joyous tones, "Papa, I think we have. I feel that I do love Jesus and trust in Him, and so do Max and Lulu, I believe."

"I do," said Max with feeling. "I know I am very, very far from perfect, but I do desire above everything else to be a follower of Jesus, and known as such; to live near Him; and honor Him in all my words and ways."

"My boy, nothing could have made me happier than that confession from your lips," his father said with emotion. "And it is no less a joy of heart to me to know that my dear, little Gracie is a follower of Jesus." He drew her nearer as he spoke, then turned loving, questioning eyes upon Lulu.

"Papa," she said in tremulous tones, "I—I feel that I am not worthy to be called one of Jesus' own disciples, but I do love Him and long to grow in likeness to Him. I do ask Him very, very often to take away all the evil that is in me and make me just what He would have me to be."

"And He will hear your prayer. He will grant your petition," her father replied in moved tones. "Oh, my dear children, your father's heart is full of thankfulness that he has reason to hope and believe that you are all true followers of the blessed Master, and that we may all live and love together, not in this world only, but also in the next."

To Max that delightful day and evening seemed very short. He was surprised when his father, glancing at his watch, said, "It is half-past nine, my son. Say good night and goodbye to your friends here, for we must go back to the Academy. It ne not be a very sad parting," he added with a smile. "As you expect to see some, if not all, of us next month at the time commencement exercises."

"Thank you, papa. That is good news," said the lad, his countenance brightening very much. "For it is the greatest treat to a fellow to see home folks once in a while."

"I know that, my boy. I haven't forgotten what it feels like to be a cadet. Your feelings are pretty much like those of other lads."

The farewells were quickly spoken, father and son entering the waiting rowboat, and in a few minutes they were at the Academy.

Captain Raymond bade his son goodbye at the door, reminding him in cheerful tones that he might hope to see him, and perhaps the entire Woodburn family, again in a few weeks.

With that prospect in view, Max went to his room in excellent spirits. He found Hunt already there.

"Hello, Max! Glad to see you back again," he exclaimed in a tone of hearty good will. "Had a royal time of it, I suppose?"

"Delightful!" cried Max merrily. "And the best of it is that my father holds out the prospect of another visit from our whole family at the time of the June commencement, which you know is not very far off."

"Well, I must say you're a lucky dog, Raymond," returned Hunt. "I wish I had the same prospect of seeing my folks, but they're too far off, and money's too scarce."

Violet was alone on deck when her husband returned to the yacht, the others having retired to the cabin or their staterooms.

"Waiting for me, love?" he asked, as he stepped to her side and passed an arm round her waist.

"Yes," she said. The air is so pleasant here, and I thought it would be really delightful for us two to have the deck entirely to ourselves for a while."

"Nothing would be more pleasant to me, my dearest," he said, his arm to his wife and beginning a leisurely promenade around the perimeter of the *Dolphin*.

"You have left Max at the Academy again?" she said interrogatively. "How manly he grows, the dear fellow, and so handsome! He's a son to be proud of, Levis."

"So his father thinks," returned the captain with a low, happy, little laugh. "My dear boy is one of God's good gifts to me."

"And how evidently he admires and loves his father—as he well may, I think. He grows more and more like you in looks, too, Levis. I can imagine that at his age you were just what he is now."

"No, my dear. He is both a more handsome and a better lad than his father was at the same age."

"Doubtless not half so conceited and vain as his father was then or is now," she returned with her low, sweet, silvery laugh. "There must have been a vast improvement, however, before I had the happiness of making his acquaintance."

"Max's?" he queried with mock gravity.

"The acquaintance of Max's father, sir," she replied demurely. "I have known the captain now for five years, and I can truly say I have never seen him show such vanity and conceit as you are pleased to charge him with, or at least to say were once among his attributes, and I will not have him slandered, even by you."

"Very well, then, let us change the subject."

"Agreed. How soon do we leave Annapolis to pursue our homeward way?"

"A little after midnight, if that plan suits my wife's wishes."

"Entirely. But you are not going to remain on deck till then?"

"Probably. I feel no inclination for sleep at the present, and the air outside here is, as you remarked a moment since, delightful."

"Especially when enjoyed in such good company, I presume?"

"Yes, that makes a difference, of course, yet I can hardly ask you to stay very long with me, cannot have the cruelty to rob my heart's best treasure—my young and lovely wife—of her beauty sleep."

"What a gallant speech!" she laughed. "It surely deserves the reward of at least another half hour of her delectable society. Ah my best and dearest of husbands," she added in a more serious tone, "there is nothing else in the world I so keenly enjoy as these rare times when I can have you all to myself."

"Yet I cannot believe they are more enjoyable to you than to me, my love," he returned. "Sweet as your society was to me in the days of courtship, it is, I think, even sweeter now. And I hope mine is not less enjoyable to you."

"Indeed, no," she said earnestly. "You seem to grow dearer and more lovable every day we live together. Oh, I can never cease to marvel that I have won so great a prize in the matrimonial lottery."

"It is wondrous strange," he returned with a happy laugh, "that a young, beautiful girl, belonging to one of the very best families in the land and who might have had her pick and choice among its most desirable matches, should have been able to secure a middle-aged widower with three children. You may well wonder at so great good fortune falling to your lot, lady mine," with a strong emphasis upon that last word.

"My husband, you could hardly bestow upon me a sweeter name than that," she said softly and with a bright, winsome look up into his face. "It is so sweet to belong to you and to have you belong to me. And our darling children are such treasures."

"Yes, our two dear babies."

"Ah, yes. But I meant to include the others also. For I surely may claim now that even Lulu loves me, not as a mother exactly, but as a dear, older sister."

"Yes, I am certain of it, dearest," he said in tones expressing heartfelt happiness. "She shows it in many ways. However many and serious her faults may be, hypocrisy and deceit are not among them."

"No, indeed! I never knew anyone more perfectly free from those faults—so perfectly open and candid. I am sure that if her life were in peril she would not be deceitful or untrue in order to save it."

"Thank you, my love," he said with emotion. "I share that belief, and it has been a great consolation to me when I have been sorely distressed by her very serious faults."

"But she is overcoming those under her father's wise and affectionate training."

"I think she is," he said. "She is most certainly struggling hard against them, though the training you speak of, has, I fear, been far from faultless."

"Ah, you have not so much confidence in her father's wisdom as I have," returned Violet with a smile and look up into his face which expressed a world of loving appreciation.

The conversation then turned upon other themes not unsuited to the sacredness of the day. They seated themselves and sang a hymn or two together, then Violet went below and sought her berth, to be followed an hour later by her husband.

Chapter Eighteenth

The next morning the *Dolphin's* passengers, upon awaking, found her speeding on her homeward way. No one regretted it, for all were full of joy at the thought of seeing home again— delightful as had been their sojourn at lovely Viamede and on the vessel.

It was still early in the day when they reached their wharf, but carriages from Ion, Fairview, and Woodburn were in waiting, and in a very short time they had left the city behind and were whirling rapidly over the familiar road toward loved homes they had left some months before—a happy company.

The grounds belonging to each estate were looking their loveliest, and the returning travelers were greeted with the warmest welcomes. Zoe and Edward had reached Ion some days in advance of the others and seen to it that everything there was in perfect order, while at Woodburn such matters had received careful attention from Christine and Alma.

"Welcome home, my love," the captain said to his wife as the carriage turned in at the great gates. "You, too, my darlings," addressing his children. "Is it almost as lovely here as at Viamede?"

"Yes, indeed, papa!" they responded, and baby Ned added, "Oh, me so blad to det home adain."

Then a joyous bark was heard, and Prince, Max's dog, came bounding to meet them.

"Oh, dere our big doggie Prince!" cried Ned with a joyous laugh and clapping his chubby hands. "Maxie dere, too, papa?"

"No, Neddie boy. We have left Brother Maxie behind at Annapolis," answered his father. Then as the carriage came to a standstill, he threw open the door, exclaiming, "Home at last!" sprang to the ground and proceeded to hand out his wife and his four children.

"Yes," said Violet, who, as well as the children, had been gazing with delight upon the grounds from the carriage window, "and I for one am as glad as I was to see Viamede on our arrival there. How very lovely everything is looking! Ah, Christine and Alma," as the two came hurrying out to greet the returned travelers, "I hope you are well? What good care you have taken of everything in our absence."

"Many thanks, Mrs. Raymond. It is very kind of you to notice it, and we are delighted to see you all at home again," the two women returned, smiling with pleasure over the arrival and Violet's appreciative words, to which the captain added his hearty commendation and the children their own glad, warm greetings.

Prince's actions, in the meantime, told the same story of his feelings. He was fawning upon one and another, capering about and wagging his tail with many a joyous bark that seemed to say, "I am very glad, very happy to see you all here again," and receiving much loving stroking and patting in return.

The servants, too, came crowding about with smiling faces and exclamations of joy and thankfulness. "Bress de Lawd you's all safe home agin!" "We's pow'ful glad to see you, cap'n, Miss Wi'let, an' all ob de chillens!"

"Dis chile 'specs yo's pow'ful hungry, Miss Wi'let an' de res', but de dinnah's mos' ready fo' to dish up," remarked the cook.

"Oh, we are not starving, by any means, Aunt Judy," returned Violet. "We had an excellent and abundant breakfast onboard the *Dolphin*, and it is hardly the regular dinner hour yet."

"Oh, papa, mayn't we run about everywhere and look at everything?" asked Lulu and Gracie almost breathlessly in their excitement.

"Certainly, daughters," he replied, smiling quite affectionately into the eager upturned faces. "Though as dinner is nearly ready, I think it might be well to first take off your hats and make yourselves neat for the table then keep within doors until after the meal."

"Oh, yes, sir," cried Lulu. "And there is no place we want to see more than our own rooms. So come, Gracie, let's hurry up there. Hark! There's my Polly screaming 'Lu! Lu!' She seems to know I've gotten home. Who can have told her? And where's your kitten, Gracie?"

"Here," returned her sister. "Don't you see I've got her in my arms? And I do believe she's glad to see me. Oh, you pretty pet! I often wanted to see you while I was away."

They were hurrying up the stairs while they talked and presently reached their own sitting room. "Oh," they cried in a breath, "how sweet and lovely it does look!" Then they made a hasty circuit of Lulu's bedroom and the little tower room that opens into it, exclaiming again and again at the beauty of the furnishings, as though they had never seen them before, and the extreme neatne which attested the good housekeeping of Christine.

Last of all they entered Gracie's bedroom, to find its appea quite as inviting as the others.

"How sweet it does look, Lu!" exclaimed Gracie. "Oh, I do think we have just the sweetest home, as well as the dearest, kindest father in the whole world!"

"Of course, we have," returned Lulu. "I would a thousand times rather be his child than any king's daughter."

"Would you, indeed, my dear child?" asked a familiar voice close behind her, while a kind hand was laid upon her shoulder. "Well, my darlings, contentment is better than wealth, and most assuredly your father would not exchange you for any king's daughters or the children of any other man."

As he spoke, he bent down to press a fatherly kiss upon Lulu's lips, then putting an arm round Gracie, caressed her in like manner.

"Now make yourselves neat for the dinner table, daughters," he said. "After the meal, if you wish, you may spend the whole afternoon in going over the house and grounds."

"Oh, thank you, papa," the exclaimed, looking full of delight.

"Lu! Lu!" called Polly from the sitting room. "What you 'bout? Polly wants a cracker."

"Oh, Polly, I beg your pardon, but you have been so quiet ever since I came in that I really forgot about you," laughed Lulu, running toward the cage, followed by her father and Gracie. "So you want a cracker, do you?"

"You shall have it, Polly," the captain said, opening the door of a small cupboard where things of that sort were wont to be kept. "Yes, here is a paper of them," taking one out and handing it to the parrot, who promptly took it in one claw, and, standing on the other foot, began biting off bits and disposing of them with a comical serious air and evident enjoyment.

Just then the little ones came running in, eager to see Polly and r her talk. But she was too much absorbed with her cracker to ʾsafe them a single word.

ʾamma ready for dinner, Elsie?" the captain asked presently.

"Yes, sir," answered Violet's own voice from the doorway. "And there is the bell."

"Then we will go down at once," said the captain, picking up Elsie and Ned and following his wife down the stairs, Lulu and Gracie bringing up the rear of the little group.

The dining room looked very attractive as they entered it. There was perfect neatness and order, vases of freshly cut flowers stood here and there, delighting the senses with their beauty and fragrance and forming a lovely decoration for the table, which presented a most inviting appearance thus ornamented and set out with delicate china, snowy damask, and glittering cut glass and silverware.

Everyone regarded it with evident satisfaction, Violet saying merrily, "After all, my dear, can any lovelier or better place be found than this—our own sweet home?"

"There is no dearer spot on earth to me, my love," he answered with a smile that spoke fond affection and delight in her appreciation of his efforts for her happiness and enjoyment.

"I think no place on earth could ever be more beautiful than Viamede," remarked Lulu. "But this is more charming because it is our very own."

"Yes," chimed in Gracie. "Papa's and mamma's and ours. It is ever so good of you, papa, to let us own it, too."

"Ah?" he returned laughingly. "But that is because I own you, you know."

He lifted baby Ned to his high chair, and now all seated themselves and the blessing was asked.

They were a lively, happy little dinner party—the children allowed a share in the conversation.

"Papa," asked Gracie at length, "are we to begin lessons tomorrow?"

"No," he replied. "I will give you two days to run about and see everything here, at Ion, Fairview, the Oaks, and so forth. Then you must settle down to work and be very good and industrious if you want to be of the Annapolis party in June."

"Oh, that will be so delightful, papa, and we do intend to be as good and industrious as possible!" she exclaimed. Lulu added, "I am sure I do, and if I should deserve punishment, papa," she went on in an undertone hardly audible to anyone but him, for as usual she was seated close at his right hand, "please do make it something else than being left at home."

"I have little fear of being compelled to punish you in that way or any other, daughter," he replied, giving her a loving look.

"Thank you, dear papa. It is kind of you to say that, and Gracie and I do just love to belong to you," raising her voice a little. "Don't we, Gracie?"

"I do, I'm sure," returned Gracie with a loving smile up into her father's face.

"Well, what shall we do this afternoon?" queried Violet. "I for one feel inclined to go all over the house and grounds and look at every dear and familiar spot."

"Well, my dear, then that is what we will do," responded her husband. "And the children may go with us or refrain, as they please," with a smiling glance from Lulu to Gracie, which both answered with an eagerly expressed desire to accompany him and Violet. Gracie added, "But I do want to see Elf and Fairy more than anything else."

"Well, dear child," said her father, "they are now disporting themselves out yonder in the meadow, and you may run out to look at and pet them as soon as we leave the table, if you wish."

"Oh, thank you, papa. That is just what I'd like to do!" she replied.

"And I think all the rest of us will be glad to go with you," said Violet.

Ned, however, presently began to nod, and he had to be carried away to his crib before the others were quite ready to leave the table.

"I think Elsie, too, looks as if she would enjoy a nap more than anything else," remarked the captain with a kind look at his youngest daughter, who seemed to be very nearly nodding over her plate.

"Oh, no, papa!" she said straightening up and opening her eyes very wide. "Please, I want to see the ponies first."

"Very well, so you shall, and the nap can come afterward," he returned in an indulgent tone.

"Then, as we are all done eating, shall we not go at once, my dear?" asked Violet.

"I think it would be well to do so," he returned. "Put on your hats, children, and we will go."

Elf and Fairy seemed glad to see their young mistresses, who stroked, patted, and fed them with bits of sugar. The next thing was to explore every nook and corner of the grounds, which to them all looked lovelier than ever.

Then they returned to the house, little Elsie willingly submitted to being laid in her crib, for she was very sleepy. And the captain, Violet, Lulu, and Gracie went over the whole house, finding it in beautiful order and saying to each other that it seemed a sweeter home than ever.

By that time there were callers from Ion, the Oaks, Roseland, and the Laurels—those from Ion bringing the news that Grandma Elsie invited all to a family reunion to be held at her home on the afternoon and evening of the next day. An invitation that every member of the Woodburn family was glad to accept.

"Ah, Brother Levis," said Rosie coaxingly, "you surely will not be so unkind as to require lessons of us tomorrow?"

"No, little sister, tomorrow and the next day may be given up amusement, but after that I shall hope and expect to have some industrious pupils."

"As you certainly shall," she replied. "I am glad of the promised holiday and am duly grateful for it, too, as I presume all your scholars are."

"Yes, yes, indeed we are, sir!" was the hearty response from Evelyn and Walter. Lulu and Gracie adding, "And so are we, papa."

The callers left early, declining an invitation to stay to tea. The family partook of their evening meal, and Gracie and the little ones, wearied with their journey, the excitement of the homecoming, and seeing so much company, went early to bed. An errand took the captain into the village for a short season, and Violet and Lulu were left for an hour or more to each other's society.

They were on the veranda together, pacing slowly back and forth—each with an arm about the other's waist.

"Oh, Mamma Vi, isn't it just delightful to be at home again?" exclaimed Lulu.

"Yes, indeed! When the home is such a one as ours and with such a man as your father at the head of affairs," returned Violet. "Lu, dear, I'm so glad that you and all his children love him as you do, though really I do not see how any one of you could help it."

"Nor do I, Mamma Vi, and I'm very glad that you love him so, too. That makes me love you even better than I could if you didn't appreciate him so highly. But we can't love him so dearly without loving one another, can we?"

"No, certainly not. I am very fond of all five children as well as of their father," Violet replied with her low, sweet laugh.